THE DRAGON'S SECOND CHANCE OMEGA

THE DRAGON'S SECOND-CHANCE OMEGA

DARKVALE DRAGONS #2

CONNOR CROWE

AN MPREG PARANORMAL ROMANCE

When the kids are away, the mates will play...
Sign up here for your FREE copy of ONE KNOTTY
NIGHT, a special story that's too hot for Amazon!
https://dl.bookfunnel.com/c1d8qcu6h8

Facebook:
fb.me/connorcrowempreg

CONTENTS

"You want a date? Fine. I'll give you a date. I'll go with you to the Rose Festival—on one condition."

"And what's that?" I threw back, waiting for the answer. The fact that he was playing along at all stunned me.

"Best me in a duel." Marlowe said it so casually, with a quirk of his lips into a wicked smile. He knew he was pushing my buttons, and he loved it.

I sputtered as I looked him up and down. Even though we'd been friends throughout our childhood, Marlowe had always been the strong one. Especially after he presented as Alpha.

"Those are the terms. Better get to practicing, Nik." Marlowe turned and went back to chopping wood. The conversation was over. I watched for a few seconds longer, eyeing the rippling muscles and the way they moved as he swung the axe through blocks of wood. A fine sheen of sweat made his skin shine in the sunlight, and made my own mouth dry.

I'd finally done it. I'd finally asked him out.

He didn't say no, but...

Another log split in half with the force of his mighty axe. I swallowed and snapped my gaping mouth shut. I knew Marlowe was strong, but seeing it like this was getting my dragon fifty shades of flustered. How would I ever beat someone like him in a duel?

I shoved my hands in my pockets and turned on my heel, away from my friend and the other alphas working nearby. It was a nice enough day, sunny with just a hint of breeze. The blood-red banners of the Firefang Clan rippled against the stone walls just like they always had. I headed off toward the Clan Alpha's quarters with a thought. He'd know what to do.

I chewed my lip as I made my way across town. I couldn't stop replaying the scene in my mind. Marlowe hadn't said no. I had to remind myself of that. And that thought alone both thrilled and terrified me. I'd only been crushing on him since forever, but nothing I did seemed to get his attention. When he joined the army, I saw him less and less. I thought my chance was gone.

But he'd returned to station in Darkvale at the request of Clan Alpha Lucien, and I saw my chance. Normally it would be unusual for an omega to make the first move, but no one had ever called me usual. And for a man like Marlowe, it was easier to kill a man than reveal his true feelings. I had to give him something to work with.

Even when we were kids, Marlowe had always been like this. Teasing, play fighting, always competitive, always looking for a win.

Would he win here as well?

My steps soon led to the Clan Alpha's chambers deep within the fortress of Darkvale.

Though Clan Alpha Lucien was an alpha, he was friendly with everyone. He ruled the Firefangs with his mate Caldo, always looking out for the elderly, the children, the omegas. It was through these overlooked peoples, Lucien was known to say, that we make true progress.

I raised my hand to the solid wooden door to knock when I heard a breathy sigh from within. I drew back my hand, embarrassed.

Guess I can just come back later...

Still frozen, still blushing, I heard Lucien's voice ring out just as I was about to make a run for it.

"Come on in, Nikolas."

"It's not urgent. I can come back if I'm interrupting..." My voice stuck in my throat like honey. Lucien wasn't at his usual haunt and the door to his private chamber was closed. What did I think was gonna happen?

Footsteps echoed on the other side of the door and the latch opened with a creak. Lucien opened the door a crack and smiled. "Not at all, come on in."

Both he and Caldo were clothed and other than the slight twinkle of a shared secret in their eyes all seemed normal.

"Thanks," I mumbled as I sunk into one of the huge cushions Lucien kept around as chairs.

"What's on your mind?" Lucien asked. He faced away from me, digging into a cabinet and making quite the racket. A small cacophony later, he fished out a few cups and filled them with spirits from a decanter nearby. "Sit, drink. Let's talk."

That's what I liked about Lucien. Despite being busy with his duties as both Clan Alpha and Caldo's mate, he always had time to speak to one of his clansmen. In the Firefangs, we were family.

"I did it," I said after taking a sip of the bracing liquor. "I asked Marlowe on a date."

"Did you now?" Lucien's eyes lit up and he gave me a toothy grin. He pulled up a chair and sat on it backward, his chin resting on the back as he straddled the seat. "Took you long enough. How did it go?"

I rolled my eyes and pursed my lips. "I'm not quite sure, actually. It was kinda awkward."

"But he didn't say no?"

"He didn't."

"What did he say, then?"

I buried my face in my hands, skin burning. "He wants to fight me. He said he'd go with me to the Rose Festival if I could beat him in a duel. Does he not see how impossible that is?"

Caldo burst out laughing from across the room.

"What?" I asked, a little annoyed. I didn't come here to get laughed at!

Caldo sniffed and caught his breath. "Typical Marlowe," he said, shaking his head. "Type A alpha if I ever did meet one. What he means, Nik, is that he likes you. He wouldn't offer that to just anyone."

I blinked, considering the prospect. "Really? Why couldn't he just say so?"

"He's a stubborn one, that's for sure. But you knew that already. I'm willing to bet that under that rough and tough exterior he sees something in you. He just doesn't know how to say it."

My heart thudded in my chest as a thrill surged through me. It seemed too good to be true. My best friend. Could we really be more?

"I'll never be able to beat him," I whined. "He knows that, too. He's so strong!"

Lucien grinned, showing all his teeth. He had a plan. "Who said strength was the only way to win? What do you say to a little training with Caldo and I?"

I swallowed the lump of anxiety in my throat and in its stead rose a swell of gratitude. What would I do without them? "You think it will work?" I asked, raising an eyebrow. My whole friendship with Marlowe was on the line, and by asking him out I'd opened Pandora's Box of Feels. No going back.

"Let's get you your man," Caldo said, and took my hand.

———

"Alphas like Marlowe are all lumbering muscle. But you have something he doesn't." Lucien circled around me, locked into a fighting stance. "I don't know if you've noticed, but that guy is a solid brick of a man. Let's just say I'm glad he's on our side."

"So how do I beat him?"

"You wear him down, just like you're gonna do here. You dodge and weave. He won't be able to keep up and when he tires, you'll have him right where you want him."

"Grab 'im by the balls!" Caldo suggested from the sidelines, eyebrows waggling. "Works every time!"

Lucien rolled his eyes. "Or you can be like Caldo and play dirty."

I had to laugh at that. "I just don't understand this whole duel thing. Why can't he just say what he means?" All this seemed awfully over the top for something as simple as a date.

"This is just how he processes things. He's never been so good with emotion, you know that."

"I wish he could say that." My shoulders slumped.

"I bet he wishes he could too."

A smile crept over my face. He had a point.

"Now come on, we've got a lot of work to do if you're gonna beat his alpha ass tomorrow!"

My heart thudded faster and fire surged through my veins. My dragon thundered within my chest, relishing the idea of being so physical with Marlowe after all these years. Grappling with my friend, falling down into the dirt together, tumbling over and over as Marlowe grabbed me and held me close...it was enough to rouse my cock right then and there.

"Save that for the battle," Lucien teased, noticing my faraway glance.

I blushed and swiped away the thoughts, but my dragon was persistent. I couldn't believe I was going through with this.

"Now come at me," Lucien taunted. "And focus!"

———

I'd never been so sore in my life. Every muscle ached, pushed to their limits. The training Lucien and Caldo put me through was merciless, but they assured me it would turn the tides in my favor. I lay in bed like an invalid, staring at the ceiling as my limbs throbbed. If I was too sore to fight, it wouldn't matter anyway.

I stared out the small window into the clear night sky. The moon was full tonight—that boded well. I whispered a prayer to Glendaria and tugged the covers around me.

Best me in a duel. The smile and glint of his eyes still rang through my mind. Tomorrow would change everything.

———

Things not to do on the day your crush wants to fight you for a date: oversleep and show up late.

Things I did: just that.

I woke up in a panic, throwing the covers off and stumbling out of bed as soon as I saw the sun in the sky. Much higher than expected. I was late.

Way to impress your crush, Nik.

I threw on some clothes and rushed out the door, sprinting to Marlowe's place. I knew the path by heart but this time it carried with it a tension that hadn't been there before. I wasn't going to Marlowe's to hang out with my buddy like we always did. I was going to fight him. To prove to him I could be his mate.

Could I?

And if it didn't work out…what then?

I shivered. Best not to think of that.

Marlowe was there waiting for me when I arrived, a knowing grin on his face. He looked me up and down as I panted. We hadn't even gotten started and I was already out of breath. His lips quirked up at the corners and he pushed away from the wall he leaned on. "Good to see you could make it. Thought you'd changed your mind."

"Never."

His eyes flashed. "You still wanna do this, then?"

I took a deep breath, appraising my friend. If all went well here today, we would be more than just friends. Maybe even mates.

"I do. And when I win, you're gonna take me to the Rose Festival." The cockiness in my voice belied the nervousness that shook me to my core. I hoped he wouldn't notice. Beneath the fear and jitters there was something else, too—a feral, consuming heat that threatened to destroy me. My dragon knew what he wanted, and he wanted Marlowe. Bad.

Marlowe raised an eyebrow. "Watch your words, omega. You better be able to back those up." He threw me a cocky grin and led me inside.

A large open space spread out before us. Nothing to get in our way. Nothing to hide behind, either.

We'd always been like this, I mused as I followed him. Always teasing, always taunting one another. But this time, the stakes were higher. Much higher.

"Rules?" I asked as I joined him in the center of the room.

"Human form only. No shifts, no weapons. Winner is first to make the other yield. Other than that?" He grinned wickedly. "Anything goes."

Anything. I swallowed the words as the idea shot straight down my spine to my cock. The deep timbre of Marlowe's taunting voice worked its way into my heart like honeyed wine, stoking the flames of passion there. The time to act was now. No more stealing glances. No more teasing one another like children. If this was what it took to prove myself, then this was what I'd do.

I drew in a deep breath through my nose and blew it out, stretching my still-sore limbs. If my hormones got the best of me now, I'd lose for sure.

"Fair enough," I replied, balling my hands into fists.

Marlowe rolled his neck and cracked his knuckles. "Let's do this. You and me, Nik. Come on!"

I said a quick prayer to the goddess Glendaria and adopted a fighting stance, trying to remember what Lucien and Caldo had taught me. Trying to access thoughts felt like wading through mud. Adrenaline, lust, and terror had shut down all rational thought and clouded my mind, leaving me alone. I had to act.

Marlowe growled and ripped his shirt off. The fabric fell away, showing the firm abs and the bulging muscles in the dim light. My mouth went dry at the sight and my dragon cried, desperate for release. I gulped.

"See something you like, Nik?" Marlowe held out his arms. "Come and get it then."

Didn't have to tell me twice. My dragon pulled me forward, ready for a fight.

Marlowe lunged toward me and swiped the air with his huge hands. I dodged at the last second, ducking beneath his grip like I'd learned. It became a sort of dance, weaving and dodging my way out of each advance. This worked my attacker into an even more feral frenzy. I was no longer his best friend Nik. I was prey.

"Come back here and fight!" He roared, lumbering toward me. "Stop moving around!"

I ducked into a roll and regained my feet behind him. Then I had an idea. I barreled into him, throwing all my weight into the lunge. This caught him off balance and we both went down, crashing into the ground on top of one another. His heated skin, slick with sweat, slipped out of my grip and Marlowe took advantage, grabbing me and flipping me over.

The wind rushed out of my lungs and I wheezed, staring up at him with wide eyes. He was huge. Marlowe hovered over me and blocked out the light, his eyes alight with the adrenaline of battle.

In that moment, I did the only thing I could think to do. I wriggled my hands free, grabbed his head, and kissed him.

To my surprise, Marlowe didn't flinch away in disgust. Instead he took control and forced his lips over mine, biting and sucking at the swollen skin there. He delved his tongue into my mouth and around my own. A deep, shuddering moan rumbled free.

"What are you doing?" I breathed.

"Pressing my advantage," Marlowe rumbled. "Anything goes, remember?"

I growled and swung my legs to the side of his torso, pulling him away from me. We tumbled together and then I was on top again, grabbing his wrists and pinning him down. It took all my weight and strength, but I straddled his chest and held him immobile for a few precious seconds.

My cock pressed through my trousers and into his chest, looking for that delicious friction.

"Someone's a little excited," Marlowe noted.

"And you're not?" I quipped. I ground my hips against him, reveling in the hot and heavy groans coming from my alpha.

I sunk down and kissed the area between his neck and shoulder, scraping my teeth against the flesh there. Goddess, he smelled like heaven. Iron and fire and musk. Wings itched at my shoulder blades, aching to come out. I bit my lip and suckled at him harder.

He could have easily thrown me off of him. But he didn't.

"Don't tell me you knew this would happen?" I asked between my little love bites.

"Fuck you," Marlowe spat and turned the tables, twisting his arms out of my grip at last.

"Fuck me?" I shot back. "That wasn't part of the rules."

"It is now," he roared. Marlowe grabbed hold of my shirt and ripped it away, fabric tearing. "Yeah, like that."

The cool air brushed past my bare skin and pebbled my already-sensitive nipples. I flailed my arms and legs against him but couldn't find purchase. Finally they found their way around Mar's neck and I pulled, forcing his face down to crotch level.

"Suck it," I growled, heat burning through every pore. I couldn't think straight anymore, or maybe I never had. I needed him. Burned for him. The fight didn't matter. Quenching this raging desire did. "Suck my fucking cock." My hips thrust upward of their own volition.

"No!" Marlowe twisted his head out of the way, shuddering in my grip.

"Yes," I growled and fisted a hand through his hair. I pulled him closer, grinding against his face.

What I didn't notice was Marlowe slipping his hand down my pants. He squeezed my ass and I hissed, suddenly aware of the position we were in.

This was supposed to be a duel, a hand to hand fight. How did we end up here?

No more questions. No more reason.

Need him. Need him now.

"Take those fucking pants off, boy." Marlowe's voice took on the same steely command as it did when he trained the troops. It sent a thrill of electricity from head to foot.

"Make me," I sneered.

"I will."

He grabbed the waistband and yanked, my pants flying upward and off. My cock bounced free, already throbbing.

Marlowe pushed my legs away and leaned over me, one arm holding me down and the other ever so softly stroking my cock. Sparks flashed before my eyes as the waves of desire grew only stronger. He was winning.

Maybe I wanted that.

I struggled beneath him, but Marlowe held firm. I was no match for his raw power.

He kept up the torturous motion on my cock as it twitched beneath him. I tried to thrust my hips upward, get more, but he held me down. "What's the matter, pretty boy? Say it."

"No," I hissed through my teeth. He fisted my cock and I groaned, throwing my head backward. My back arched, my breath came in gasps. After all the nights fantasizing about something like this, nothing held a candle to what was happening right now.

"What's going on down here, I wonder?" Marlowe snaked a finger lower to my dripping hole.

"Ah, fuck!" I moaned as he probed the ring of muscle there. Goddess, it felt so good. I couldn't even imagine how he would feel within me—

"Now fight me, omega! Fight me!" Marlowe jerked away in an instant. Whiplash seized me, every pore and nerve tense and ready to spring. Mar's voice was nothing more than a feral roar, but my dragon understood every word.

Fire threatened to consume my body as we tangled together. Our bare chests and sweaty skin pressed so close made my head spin and worked my dragon into a frenzy. Fire and iron and blood and magic, he was mine, he was mine...

Mate! The dragon screeched from the depths of my soul. Mate! Mate!

I gathered my strength and pawed at Marlowe's pants, unfastening them at the waist. He didn't resist, even helped me a bit. He kicked them aside and we were right back at it, rolling around on the ground naked, grunting and straining to subdue the other. I was tiring, but so was he. The animalistic grunts, the hot pants of breath, the slick and sweaty skin kept me going.

Our hard cocks pressed into one another and our eyes were like fire. There was nothing better than this, the thought wove through my hazy mind.

I couldn't take my eyes off of Marlowe's straining cock. Sure, I'd fantasized about it more than a few times. But seeing it in person was another matter completely. I reached down and wrapped a hand around it, marveling at the girth of it. My fingers barely fit around his rod and I sucked in a breath thinking how it might feel inside of me.

Could I even take the whole thing?

"Mmmm," Marlowe let out in a low sigh as I worked my hand up and down his length. "That's nice."

Without warning he grabbed my arms and spun me around, slamming me onto my back. I coughed and looked up at him, his hulking frame hovering above me. Heat poured off of his sweaty body in waves, and more than that, the alpha pheromones he gave off were simply too good to resist. I took a long drag through my nose, letting his personal musk fill my senses.

Yes. Goddess, yes.

"Do you yield yet?" Marlowe's voice brought me back to the moment. His jaw clenched, his voice strained. He was holding himself back.

"Never," I hissed through my teeth. I wanted to egg him on. I wanted to see where this would go.

"You asked for it," my alpha growled and brought his hand to my slick, dripping opening. He coated his fingers in my juices and brought them to his nose, sniffing deeply before sucking them into his mouth.

He rumbled deep in his chest, closing his eyes as he tasted me. Goddess, that was so fucking hot. My cock twitched and strained against Marlowe's body and my breath came out in frenzied pants.

"You're so wet," Marlowe groaned. "Would be a shame not to put that to use."

I narrowed my eyes, all thought blanked out by the feeling of him on top of me, the fire raging within my soul, our dragons so close to one another, straining to meet, to play, to mate.

"Do it!" I groaned through gritted teeth. We'd reached a crescendo. A point of no return. If I was gonna tumble over this cliff, I was taking him with me.

Marlowe let out a booming draconic roar and the head of his cock speared through my channel. I gasped as it filled me, stretching beyond anything I'd felt before. Amidst the haze of momentary pain there was something else— heat. Raging, unrelenting heat.

I bucked my hips toward him, drawing his hard throbbing cock deeper into my channel. Marlowe's eyes widened and he grinned incredulously.

I sighed and threw my head back, stars dancing before my eyes. Electric currents zapped and sparkled between us, weaving an ancient connection that only true mates could experience.

"After all this time?" Mar said, his voice awed. "Why didn't you ever say anything?"

The old fears came rushing back. The old memories. "Thought you had your sights set on another," I said sheepishly, my voice deepening into a moan as he slid all the way in, balls deep in my tight channel. "Never thought you'd see me like that."

And now here they were, close as two men could be. Their sweaty bodies writhed together as one, Marlowe seating himself deep within.

"Shut up," Marlowe mumbled. He put a finger over my lips and I clicked my teeth, threatening to bite it.

Goddess, this was so fucking good. Better than flying.

Better than Myrony's best stew. Better than maple candies.

"Always you, Nik. Always you. I'm just sorry it took this long." My alpha's voice carried a hint of sadness now as he remembered some long-forgotten pain. "I was too blinded by my fears to do anything about it. Thought I could block it all out. But then you asked me, and my walls came tumbling down. I've wanted you for so fucking long."

He thrust into me again, probing the sensitive spot deep inside. I moaned and lifted my hips, straining for more.

"That makes two of us," I breathed. "Now show me that you mean it!"

We turned into a single mass of growling, sweating flesh. Marlowe drove his cock home again and again, building the tension and fire to unquenchable levels.

"Goddess, you're tight," Mar groaned, kissing my lips, my neck, my chest. He picked up the rhythm, a frantic flicker in his eyes.

"Last chance," he bit off the words as our gaze locked together. I held him there, pumping my hips and matching his thrusts. The circuit was nearly complete. "Do you yield, Nikolas Lastir?"

"Never," I said with conviction, and held him to me as he tumbled over the edge, jerking and thrusting as he came.

His knot swelled against me, locking us together as mates. The stretch made me dizzy, made me see stars. I couldn't take it any longer and groaned, thrusting beneath him. Hot gobs of cum shot over my chest, smearing onto sweaty skin.

But more than that, the sense of something greater overcame me. A celestial connection that had been forged here today, binding together our bodies, our minds, our spirits. Marlowe and Nikolas. Alpha and omega. Mates. Family.

We lay there for some time, still knotted together, still holding one another close. It took a few minutes for my breathing to return to normal. For all the sweat to dry. I fluttered open my eyelids and saw Marlowe there, gazing at me with a sleepy grin. "So how about that date?"

Marlowe laughed, tousling my hair and kissing my forehead. "Wait, who won the duel?" He furrowed his eyebrows, thinking.

"Does it matter?" I chuckled.

"You are my mate. My best friend. My confidante. There is no greater win than that."

I nuzzled into him, still sniffing at the primal musk that coated his skin. Mate. This dragon is my mate. Mine. Forever.

I snapped my eyes open, propping up on an elbow. "You knew this was going to happen."

"I did not." Marlowe held up his hands in an innocent gesture. "I had my hopes, though." He winked.

I groaned. "You're ridiculous." Try as I might, I couldn't stop the grin from spreading over my face.

"You mean ridiculously sexy?" Marlowe quipped, nudging me.

We laughed, holding one another close, knotted together both in body and soul.

"And yes, I will take you to the Rose Festival. It's a date." Marlowe rested his forehead against mine, his breath slowing as he slipped away to slumber.

Right here, in this moment, was all I ever wanted. We weren't just friends anymore. We were mates. And nothing could stop us now.

1

MARLOWE

PRESENT DAY

We had 'em by the balls.

Supply lines cut short. The fortress surrounded. It was only a matter of time.

Darkvale would be ours.

My heart raced with adrenaline and the endorphins of battle. Finally, after five years of hiding and preparing, we were fighting back. Finally, we could return home.

"Firefangs!" I roared in a lusty battle cry, fire building in my chest. The walls of Darkvale stood tall, reinforced with stone and mortar. The magical dome over the city made simply flying over the walls impossible, but we could still knock them down. And if we couldn't get in, they couldn't get out. Siege 101.

I flapped my wings harder, gaining speed, then tucked them to my side as I slammed into the wall like a torpedo.

I braced myself against the impact and it shuddered me to the bone. But the walls shuddered too, cracks of plaster and stone coming free.

"To the walls!" I cried, and my battalion followed suit around me. The sky thundered with the sound of dragons pummeling the stone walls like battering rams, over and over again.

Thank the Goddess for my armored scales, but I was starting to feel a little dizzy. In human form I'd have broken just about every bone in my body by now. But we couldn't stop just yet.

The wall was weakening.

I projected my voice, booming through the walls into the city I'd once called home. "Your time is up, Paradox! We've cut off your supply lines. We've caved in your tunnels. There is no way out. You can surrender peacefully, or we shall burn this castle to the ground!"

A few beats of blessed silence, then a shuffling sound echoed behind the walls. A sniveling voice responded.

"You wouldn't dare. Cut off your nose to spite your face? Not likely."

The high-pitched whine stirred the rage inside me even more. I caught sight of a glowing orange eye through a chink in the wall and grinned, showing off my rows of razor-sharp teeth. "Try me."

A great explosion of crumbling stone sounded to my left

and I swerved, narrowly missing the falling debris. As the dust cleared, I could see that Tork our demolitions expert had breached the wall, light spilling into the human-sized hole he'd left behind.

I wasted no time. "For Darkvale!" I called, and forced my shift down deep into my chest. It wasn't easy—my dragon was in full-on bloodlust mode—but as my hands and feet returned to normal I clawed through the breach and into my old home.

Not all of the Paradox fighters were in their shifts. The enclosed space made sure of that. I roared and lunged forward, ducking to the side as a column of fire erupted from a nearby dragon.

I heard shouts and war cries behind me, and I didn't dare chance a glance but I knew my team had followed. They poured into the city like water through a broken dam, eyes blazing with determination and fire.

"For Darkvale!" The shouts rung out, and I was filled with an arresting sort of pride.

We'd done it.

But the fight wasn't over yet.

I dodged and weaved through the morass of men and dragons, grabbing a broken wooden staff off the ground to use as a weapon. The dragon inside roared in triumph, begging to be released once more.

I tamped the feeling down, focusing only on the

makeshift spear in my hand and the flood of my enemies around me.

"Watch it, Mar!" Tork's voice carried over the storm and I swiveled around, my staff meeting the blade meant for my back. The wood vibrated with the impact and I almost dropped it. But my attacker would have liked that too much.

The rust-colored face of a Paradox fighter grinned deliriously down at me, pressing his advantage. His eyes shone a rare green instead of the standard yellow or orange. An Elemental dragon.

I dug my heels into the earth and held on. Our muscles bulged, our teeth bared in bloody grins as we fought for dominance. "Give it up, lowblood," the attacker growled.

"Never," I promised, and threw all my weight and strength into a forward lunge, throwing my attacker off balance. I took the opportunity and drove the sharpened edge of the stake deep into his stomach. He gasped and gurgled, eyes wide. In a final act of defiance the ground shook and changed, the particles vibrating under my feet. Goddess-damned Elementals!

The dirt beneath me became muddy and thin like a slop of quicksand and soon I felt myself sinking, slurping into the Earth. The Elemental was sinking, too, but he had the look of a man who knew he got in the last word. His life force drained away through his abdomen in a bloody haze, but he kept his gaze fixed on me, watching as I tried to clamber my way out of the pit.

Try as I might, I sunk only deeper, in up to my knees now. I watched with wide eyes as the battle raged around me, swords and fire and claws filling the air with the thunder of dragons. My arms scrabbled around on the dirt, looking for something, anything I could anchor myself on. Nothing came.

"Grab on!" Tork yelled and offered me a hand. It was coated in sweat and slipped through my fingers as I sank further. He desperately wiped it and leaned down.

"Pull!"

This time he held firm and I used his body as an anchor to climb free, my boots popping free of the suction-like substance with a final pop. I sprawled on the ground, staring at the sky for only a second before I was back on my feet.

"Close one there," Tork said, handing me a blade. "Fuckin' Elementals."

"He's dead," I assured him, and we rejoined the fray.

I grabbed a running officer by the collar and gave him my most intimidating roar. "Where is Arion? Where is your leader?"

The man cowed beneath my gaze but held a sickly grin that told me he knew something I didn't. I hated it.

"He's not here," the man chuckled. "You're too late."

My dragon would stay silent no longer. A feral roar ripped itself from my throat and sparked a fire, roasting the man where he stood. I dropped the charred corpse to the ground and looked around, my eyes clouded with bloodlust.

Find the leaders. Kill them. Kill them all!

Behind the red haze of battle, another ache began to take hold. A deep, heart-rending ache of nostalgia, guilt, grief.

I was home. I hadn't set foot in these walls in five years, and oh, how things had changed....how *I* had changed...

"Marlowe, we've got them!" The voice roused me from my thoughts and two of my officers approached. Two enemy Cogs in shackles sank to their knees in front of me, their tired, dusty faces full of pure hatred.

"We've got two commanding officers here. They seem to be in charge. Knox's nowhere to be found."

"Coward," I muttered and appraised the two men in front of me. They wore the silver uniforms of Paradox officials and their faces were hard, mean. They didn't meet my gaze. Didn't want to admit defeat, no doubt.

"Where is your leader?" I asked them just as I had the other soldier.

They didn't say anything for a moment, then the man on the left narrowed his eyes and peered straight at me, voice full of malice. "You think we're gonna tell you, lowblood scum?"

There was that phrase again. Lowblood.

I fought to keep my voice even. "Tell me and I might let you live."

The man spat in response, a lump of phlegm landing near my feet. I turned and left them to my officers.

"Roast them," I said casually, and walked away as the sounds of their screams echoed behind me.

My mind buzzed with a million questions, ached with a million little paper cuts. I was home, and yet...it didn't feel like I thought it would. I should have been happy.

Instead, I felt nothing.

The city grew silent save for the moaning of the fallen. The fight was over. We'd won. The stink of blood was heavy in the air, on my skin, under my scales. I rounded a corner and slumped against a stone column. My hands and face reveled in the cool, smooth surface as if I was feeling it for the first time. This courtyard was where I used to play hide and seek as a kid. I was home. Finally, I was home.

"There's no sign of Nikolas, sir." Arthur, my scout, stepped toward me. He shrugged and winced and at the same time.

I closed my eyes and let out a breath as grief washed over

me anew. Of course not. How foolish could I have been to think he'd still be here? Still be alive?

The sick, gnawing agony in my gut twisted like a knife. I was home...but without Nik, did it even matter?

That part of my life was over. Had been over, for years now. So why couldn't I get him out of my head?

"If I may, sir," Arthur started. He pulled out a handkerchief and offered it to me.

"You may not." I bit off the words and straightened, assuming the role of the cold military commander once more. Feelings had no place on a battlefield, and there was much work to be done.

"Gather the troops. I wish to speak with them."

"Right away, sir." Arthur hurried off. I stared at the dome above us, enjoying a few more seconds of peace.

———

"It is through each and every one of your efforts that we are standing here today, in the city of our forefathers. No longer shall we run and hide in fear. No longer shall we be relegated to the shadows. We've routed the Paradox. Darkvale is ours once more."

Cheers thundered through the crowd in a way that only dragons could.

"I know that if Clan Alpha Lucien were here, he would

say the same. He's had to leave on some urgent business, but has left command with me in his stead. He shall return soon, but in the meantime, let's get this place cleaned up. We want a new Darkvale to show him when he returns, you hear me?"

I looked out at the crowd of men and women I'd fought, lived, and dreamed with for the last five years. Through forests, caves, tunnels, shanties, they'd been there for me. We'd been there for each other. And we'd finally done it. At long last, we'd done it.

Darkvale was ours once more. But at what cost?

"Tonight, we will honor our fallen. Tonight, we will spend time with our families. We will hug our children. We will prepare for our new life. Tomorrow, we build."

A voice from the back spoke up. Kari, one of our strongest soldiers. "What of the survivors?" She asked. "We've dispatched the Cog officers, but there are still many villagers left within these walls. What of them?"

My heart jumped in my chest. Maybe, just maybe...Nik would be there.

"We'll give them a choice." I said finally. "They can bend the knee, or they can die."

Kari nodded in acknowledgment. I continued. "Come daybreak, Arthur will go around to each home and take note of the remaining individuals. They will need to swear fealty to Clan Alpha Lucien officially when he returns, of course, but we need to let them know the terms now so that they can make their choice. Are there any more questions?"

The crowd was quiet, shuffling back and forth on tired feet.

"Very well. You're dismissed."

The crowd dispersed, and as it did I felt the same weight of longing drape back over me like a blanket. I couldn't escape it. Sooner or later, I would have to face the facts.

The man I'd loved—the man I'd left behind—was gone.

2

NIKOLAS

The acrid scent of smoke filled the air and wove its way into my lungs. You'd think a dragon would be used to a little smoke smell, right?

But this was more than just a little smoke. It smelled like the whole city was burning. And here I was, trapped in a very-flammable house with no way out.

Those damn Paradox bastards.

A sliver of hope rose in my chest as I went around, clattering the shutters against the pollution. The sounds of steel and shouting echoed off the walls. Battle. Someone was fighting. But who? And who was winning?

The thought of finally getting out of here was tempting, but I'd learned five years ago that things rarely work out the way you expect.

The night Darkvale fell was both the best and the worst day of my life.

He was handsome. He was alpha. And he wanted me. In the midst of our passion, fire and terror rained from the sky. I didn't know it then, but it was the final mutiny that would oust Clan Alpha Lucien and bring the city under Paradox control.

I remembered him running outside to see what was going on, dressed in only a robe. He never came back. The chaos and violence tore us away from one another and I screamed myself hoarse trying to find him. No response came.

When the Paradox soldiers—they called themselves Cogs —knocked down my door, I knew it was over.

For the first few days or even weeks in captivity, I remained convinced that my mate would come back to rescue me. Even if he didn't, surely Clan Alpha Lucien would...right? I prayed to the Goddess Glendaria night and day, begging, beseeching, pleading, bargaining. Nothing worked.

Weeks stretched into months stretched into years. They never came. None of them.

Now I was trapped here in this Goddess-damned house that might as well be a prison cell. I had food, clothes, supplies, sure. But the walls were coated with a magical tar-like substance that suppressed my shift and made sure I couldn't escape.

They never physically hurt me, at least not directly. For that I was thankful. But I was no better than an animal to them, a permanent hostage, a plaything.

"Dad?" The small voice caught my ear and I turned from the window.

A four-year-old girl with pigtails looked up at me.

Oh yeah, and there was that. He'd also left me with an unplanned parting gift: a baby.

He never even knew.

I looked at her as if seeing her for the first time, all rosy cheeks and mussed hair and an innocent smile that could light up any day. She wasn't much of a baby anymore, I mused. Far from it. Lyria was four years old, nearly five, and just as spirited as her alpha father. It was a shame she never got a chance to meet him.

"Dad, what's going on?"

I stepped forward and held her close. "Nothing, sweetie. Go to your room and don't make a sound. Can you do that for me?"

She nodded, wide-eyed.

The door shook as a clattering knock echoed through the house. Someone was outside. My heart leapt into my chest.

"Go now," I whispered and she ran off without a word.

I grabbed a kitchen knife from the counter and crept toward the door, holding my breath. Not like a puny kitchen knife would do much against a dragon, but I had to try.

An image flashed through my mind as I clasped the doorknob. It was ridiculous, but I almost expected to see my lost mate on the other side, smiling wide as ever.

But it wasn't.

Of course it wasn't.

I opened the door to a man in uniform, bearing the red and gold sigil of the Firefangs. My blood ran cold at the sight. My Goddess, they'd finally done it.

"Arthur Linn here to take a census. The Firefangs have occupied Darkvale and routed the Paradox traitors. Pledge your fealty to Clan Alpha Lucien and no harm shall come to you. Refuse, and meet the dragon's justice." The officer read off of a scroll then snapped his gaze to mine. There was a flicker of recognition, or perhaps confusion. Only a moment, though.

A wave of emotion flowed through me like a storm. It was Lucien and his late mate Caldo that had helped me gain Marlowe's favor in the first place. And now Lucien was back. That could only mean...

I swallowed, flashing back to the man I'd seen from the peephole in the wall not long ago. Fire and steel and dragons raged outside, and one man in particular led them all. He stormed through the breach like nothing could stop him, bellowing as he cut down Cogs left and right. When I saw it, I thought it was a hallucination. Just my brain wanting to see my long lost mate one more time before I died.

But it was no hallucination.

Peter Marlowe had returned. After all this time, he'd returned.

Who was I to think he'd want anything to do with me? He betrayed me. He left me to raise a child alone in Paradox territory. I couldn't forgive him for that.

And yet, I couldn't ignore the stirring of hope in my heart. A part of myself still longed for him, and I hated myself for it.

"Get lost," I growled at the servant, my lip curling in disgust. The pain of Marlowe's betrayal still coursed through me, clouding my thoughts. "I'll speak to Lucien myself."

Arthur clenched his jaw and made a damning mark on his scroll. "Very well, then. I do hope you will reconsider."

With that he was gone, off to the next house. He launched into the same spiel about fealty, Lucien, and the Firefangs. I sunk down onto a chair and clapped my hands over my ears.

We were free at long last. But I never thought it would feel like this.

3

MARLOWE

I woke with the sun. Strange, feeling the sunlight on my skin once more. After so long hiding underground, everything felt so bright. So colorful.

I threw myself out of the hammock, wobbling a bit as I got to my feet. My muscles screamed with exertion and soreness.

Yesterday, we'd attacked Darkvale.

Yesterday, we'd won.

I rubbed the sleep from my eyes and hastily dressed, eager to get on with the business of the day. A lump of guilt still lodged itself deep in my heart, but I had more than enough other tasks to focus on. Rebuilding a town was no easy feat, and if what Lucien had told me was correct, we were going to have quite the population influx soon.

There was no time for grief. In Lucien's stead, people looked to me as a leader. It was my job to act the part.

I brushed my dark hair back behind my ears and threw on my officer's uniform. When I exited my quarters my servant Arthur was already there, waiting for me.

Ever vigilant, that one.

"The census, sir." He followed me to the granary, not missing a beat. He waited by my side as I shouldered a bag of rice and carried it to Myrony, who'd already begun assessing the food stores. They'd gathered a few low-hanging fruits from nearby trees and the rice along with a couple choice herbs would make a filling lunch.

I finally turned to my unwanted shadow. "I just woke, Arthur, and my dragon's starving. Can't it wait?"

Arthur's shoulders slumped. "I'm afraid it cannot. I made my rounds with the census, sir. There are a few families on the west end of town who chose not to bend the knee. At least, not yet. Whether they're Paradox sympathizers or simply stubborn mules I cannot say. But we cannot have traitors in our midst. You know what happened last time."

My stomach tightened into a knot. I tasted bile in the back of my throat. Of course I knew what happened last time. Last time, we'd lost our home. And I'd lost Nik.

"What would you have me do, Arthur?" I sighed, popping a few grapes into my mouth. The juices spread across my tongue, tangy and sweet at once. So much better than the stale rations we'd grown used to.

"I thought you might want to see to them personally."

There it was again. That tiny sliver of hope, flickering like a candle in the depths of my heart. Was Nik still out there?

"Very well," I said. "Give me the register and I'll drop by. But I'm finishing breakfast first."

Arthur nodded in response and handed over the scroll, taking his leave.

I sunk onto a bench. My joints creaked. Goddess, I hadn't had a good fight in so long. Yesterday's battle was exhilarating, to be sure, but I always seemed to forget how sore and tired I was afterward.

I propped up my head with a hand and looked to Myrony, hard at work sorting through the food and leaning over a small fire she'd started for the cooking pot.

"What do you think, My?" I asked by way of conversation.

"About what?" She asked, not taking her eyes off her work.

"All of this." I waved my hand around at the fortress. "We're finally home."

She gave me a small smile. "We are. Feels different, though, doesn't it?"

I frowned. "It does."

"Things aren't going to go back to normal, are they?" She didn't meet my gaze, staring into the cooking fire that flickered before us.

I grimaced, thinking of all the things we'd both lost. "No, they're not."

She straightened, wiping her ashy hands on her apron. "Well, eat up. You'll need your strength."

In more ways than one, I mused, and took a bite.

———

Now that I had a full stomach, I could see to the rest of the day's business. I had to meet with the builders, post guards on the walls, and follow up with Myrony on inventory. Lucien would be returning any day now, and we needed to have things well in motion before that happened. He had a mate to look after. A mate with child. It was up to us to keep things running in his stead.

And apparently, now I had to go scout out some rogue villagers as well.

This day was getting crowded already. I wiped my brow and got to work.

The meeting with the builders went swiftly—I had Tork on hand to provide a little much needed muscle. The damage done to the structure was more than we'd hoped, but the builders assured me they could have it patched up in no time. And with someone like Tork at the helm helping clear the rubble, I didn't doubt it for a second.

The walls stood firm around us, in all but the place where we'd breached them coming in. The dome above held tight, filtering air through but remaining resilient to any fire or magical attacks. Our magitech engineers, in a feat of brilliance since unmatched, built a giant dome to protect Darkvale. At least the Paradox hadn't let that go to waste, I thought grimly.

The hole in the stone wall left us exposed, though. I gathered a few of my soldiers and posted them there on watch while the builders scurried around. First priority was getting the wall patched, then they could set to restoring the buildings. Sleeping quarters, a kitchen, an armory. Our numbers were smaller than they'd ever been, but not for long. The Firefangs would rise anew.

Guards paced the walls in each cardinal direction: north, south, east, and west. If anything, man or dragon, was coming, we'd see it.

I dawdled by speaking with a few of the villagers that had emerged from their homes. Subconsciously, I was still avoiding the rogue settlement Arthur had tasked me with investigating.

But it wasn't just that, a tiny voice reminded me. *You're afraid.*

I winced, swatting the thoughts away.

Alphas don't get afraid.

This one does.

I frowned and balled my hands into fists. I wanted to punch something, anything.

No matter how much I tried to distract my mind, I couldn't avoid the inevitable. Either Nik would be there, or he would not. Somehow, delaying the task made it feel a little more possible in my mind.

Once I visited the rogues, I'd know for sure one way or another. And that was perhaps more terrifying than not knowing at all.

———

Finally, I could delay no longer. I grabbed Arthur's register and set out on foot to the west. The houses there surprised me. I hadn't remembered any villagers living here last time I was in Darkvale, but that was five years ago now. The buildings were crude but sturdy, reinforced with black tar that resisted dragon fire. I clenched my jaw.

These weren't just humble huts. They were meant to keep someone in. Or someone out.

A voice clawed through my mind, reaching through ages of forgotten cobwebs and long-lost memories.

I knew that voice. Nik's voice.

The night Darkvale fell, I failed more than just my Clan Alpha. I failed my mate. Screams and fire ripped through the air and I stepped outside for only a moment. But that moment lasted for the next five years.

I left him, alone and naked. I was forced out of the city, forced into hiding. I thought he was right behind me. I thought maybe someone else had helped him escape and we just got separated in the chaos.

When the flames died down, he was nowhere to be found. And that's when I shut myself off completely.

It wasn't quite the same as Lucien's curse. My heart didn't break that day, no. I simply built a brick wall around it, blocking out any feeling. My days and nights turned to only one thing: war. It was the only thing I knew, only thing I was good at. And somehow, I had this delirious hope that if I could just stay moving, I'd finally forget about him. I'd finally find absolution.

But that was a fool's errand. Now I was back in Darkvale. And Nik was here. I could feel it.

The whispering voice grew stronger as I approached the western settlement. They were more like prisoner cells than houses, I realized with a shiver. Is that what they'd done with him? Trapped him in a sealed house to rot, or worse?

My dragon rose within me, all fury and fire. I'm sorry, I sent out into the void. I'm sorry, I'm so sorry.

No response came.

The tall stone door of the safe house loomed before me. There were only a few small windows to let light in, but they were shuttered. *Please let this be him,* I whispered in a silent litany to Glendaria as I raised my hand to knock. *Please let him be okay.*

I pounded on the door sharply, three times. I cleared my throat, waiting for a response. None came.

I knocked again. My breath caught in my throat this time and my mouth suddenly went dry. What if he had moved on? What if—Goddess forbid—he had mated another?

"This is Peter Marlowe of Firefang command. Open up at once." I tried to keep my voice firm, commanding. It only cracked once.

A long moment passed. I was about to turn and leave when the door creaked open, and there he was.

Nikolas Lastir, my best friend. My mate. The man I'd left behind.

It was still him, all right. But the years hadn't been kind. His face showed lines of weary grief and toil, eyes deep in their sockets. His blond hair hung down past his eyebrows and he had a sort of haunted expression about him, like he'd been possessed by a ghost. Or maybe he was one.

Nik was here all right. But one look at him solidified my fears. Everything had changed.

4

NIKOLAS

I couldn't tell you how many times I'd played out this situation in my mind, hoping that it would come true.

None of those wistful daydreams prepared me for the reality.

I swallowed against the lump in my throat and gritted my teeth against the roaring of blood in my ears. There he was, flesh and blood. My alpha. My mate.

Marlowe.

He looked older, sure, and sported more than a few new battle scars. It was the look on his face that really did me in, though.

His eyes searched mine, looking for a spark of recognition, for some assurance that I was still his.

After five years of silence, did it even matter?

"What do you want?" I said finally, voice low. "What are you doing here?"

Marlowe's face fell. "I came back, Nik." His voice broke. "I told you I would. We defeated the Paradox. We're free."

My dragon roared inside me, ready to pounce. I scowled and cursed before I could censor myself. "Fuck off with that. It's been five years. I haven't heard from you once. Too little, too late."

Marlowe sagged. "I don't know what you want me to do. I didn't mean to leave you. Everything happened so quickly. I did what I had to do."

"And what about us, Mar? What about that?" The words flung like daggers, slicing through the cold silence. "You even closed off your Link." My lip curled and I watched with some perverse enjoyment the look of shock on his face. "Coward."

Marlowe bared his teeth, a growl rumbling from low in his chest. We stood there, facing off, neither of us willing to make a move.

Finally, he shoved a piece of paper at me.

"Just...sign this paper. I'll leave you alone."

In a burst of hot anger, I dropped the paper and slammed the door in his face, shoulders heaving. A burst of fire rushed through every vein, every pore, and I roared in pain.

Lyria chose this moment to emerge from her room, eyes wide and watery at her omega father's predicament.

"Daddy!" She screeched, cowering in the corner.

The sound of my little girl was enough to return me to sanity. I shook from head to toe with anger, resentment, grief, fear.

How *dare* he come back like this? How *dare* he waltz right in and think things would go back to normal? Five years, five long years I spent toiling away by myself, raising a child, living like a trapped animal under the Paradox regime. And he did nothing. Nothing!

That's when the sobs began.

Lyria ran forward and threw her arms around me, anchoring me back into reality. "Daddy, what's wrong?"

I held her close, breathing in the scent of her hair, feeling the warmth of her skin. How could I even begin to explain?

"I'm sorry, sweetheart," I whispered and rubbed her back. "I'm sorry. Everything's all right."

"Who was that man?" She asked and felt me tense beneath her. I let out a breath. My eyes stared off into space.

I didn't respond. Couldn't. She didn't press, thank Glendaria for that. We sat there together, holding one another and crying for all the things we'd lost.

It wasn't fair, my mind screeched at me. She didn't deserve this. She needed a happy, normal childhood. But after five years in captivity, what did normal even mean anymore?

And Marlowe...Goddess, Marlowe. He didn't even know he had a daughter. I wasn't even sure I wanted him to know now. My mind fought in all directions, the mate connection clashing with the hurt and betrayal in my heart.

Did he forget about me? Did he never even care?

Whatever the reason, I had this little one to take care of. I sniffed away my tears and held Lyria tight. She was my beacon of hope in this war-torn world, and no one, not even Marlowe, would take that away from me.

5

MARLOWE

I needed to fly.

Wings sprouted from my back and I leapt into the air, my strong back legs kicking off the ground. I couldn't go too high while the dome was in place, but I needed that space. Needed some air to breathe.

Raw emotion still flooded through me, searing at my hardened heart.

Coward.

The word burned itself into my chest like a brand, and I couldn't fly fast enough to escape it.

After five long years, I found him. I found my mate. He was alive, but his face had long lost the innocent gleam it once had. They had trapped him here like some kind of animal.

And I did nothing.

Just like the first time he confessed his feelings for me. I didn't know how to handle it then, and I sure didn't know how to handle it now. Last time, I ended up challenging him to a duel as a way to sort things out.

A very *sexy* duel, as it turned out.

A small grin broke out over my face as I remembered that moment. We went into it facing off like warriors, but our dragons wanted more than just a good fight. We fucked right then and there, sweat and muscle and panting breaths as we struggled for control, for dominance. It was the hottest sex I'd ever had.

Today I'd made the same mistake. By shoving away my feelings I'd hurt the person that meant most to me. He made me smile on my bad days, he brought light to my otherwise mundane life. At least, he did.

Now? I wasn't sure of anything anymore.

If today was any indication, he didn't want anything to do with me. That was fair. I was the one that left him trapped and alone. I could have tried to reach out to him. I could have done something to help. But could I have done it without compromising the clan's security?

Too late now.

I flapped my wings harder, ascending up to the level of the dome. Looking down on Darkvale made me feel a little better. Pride and patriotism covered the hurt for the briefest moment. The same walls and buildings I grew up in still stood. Men and women moved about the keep with purpose, each with a task to do. The builders gathered stone and mortar to repair the wall, Myrony and a group of helpers gathered food and supplies, and guardsmen paced the walls with sharp eyes, looking for any sign of movement.

This was my family. This was my home. All those years of hiding, of war, of fighting. This was what we fought for. We were home once more.

I settled on the ground next to the officer's quarters, shifting back into human form before entering. The men startled as I stepped in, looking up from a map spread out over a table.

"Commander Marlowe," Bryn stood and saluted. The other men did the same. All pesky formality, really.

"We've received reports of Sorcerers nearby, and I don't like the look of it."

I froze, panic twisting in my gut. Sorcerers. The very same that had captured Lucien's mate?

"What are they doing so close to our territory?" I asked, peering at the map they had laid out.

A small red x marked the spot, a valley not three miles from here shielded on all sides by cliffs. Also a perfect place to ambush them, should we wish to.

"Send out a few scouts for reconnaissance. I want to know why they're there and what they're planning. Do not engage, unless in self defense. We need to keep on our guard."

"Very well." Bryn nodded.

"Any other news from the field?" I asked, pacing around to my seat at the head of the table. I clasped my hands together and rested my chin on them. I had no taste for war-room meetings right now. Not after being snubbed by Nik. But I tried to keep my voice interested, or at least formal. They depended on me.

"None," my officer Rayn added. "With your permission, we'd like to send an engineer over to the west end and remove the enchantments trapping the villagers there. You have confirmed their loyalty?" He looked at me with a question in his eyes.

My stomach seized into a knot again and I squeezed my eyes shut for a moment. Loyalty? Not quite, but treason? I didn't think Nik was capable of that either. If he didn't want to deal with me, fine. But he still owed himself to Lucien and the clan. "Yes," I said after a long breath. "Release them, thank you."

Rayn gestured to3 our chief engineer. "It will be done, sir." He stood and left.

"If that's everything?" I asked hopefully, rising from the chair. I needed to be alone right now.

"It is."

"You're dismissed." I waved a hand and they dispersed,

muttering among themselves. I tried not to think about the looks of concern on their faces.

After the officer's meeting I wandered around Darkvale for a bit longer, checking in on the status of the builders, the gatherers, the hunters. When I could find no further diversions, I returned to my quarters and sunk into my hammock, staring up at the afternoon sky.

Clouds floated by in wisps of white, casting long shadows on the walls and people within them. The dome covering Darkvale refracted the light and shone rays of color down onto the ground, shimmering in the daytime sun.

All was going swimmingly. All except the matter of Nikolas, that was.

My stomach gurgled loudly. Myrony would start in on dinner soon, and perhaps if I went to help I could sneak a few bites before the bell. I knew that once dinner came, however, I'd have to face the villagers once again. I'd have to face him.

Of course they'd bring all the clansmen together for food. Why wouldn't they? We were family, after all. Firefangs were family. Not by blood, no, but by choice.

And our family was about to get bigger. Over two dozen villagers had stayed behind after we took Darkvale from the Cogs and pledged themselves to Clan Alpha Lucien. We'd have a proper ceremony once he returned, of course, but tonight we'd break bread with them for the first time.

I thought again about the engineers on their way to release the enchanted holding houses. Nik was in one of them, and that meant he would be at dinner too.

How long had they kept him in there? I furrowed my brow. I didn't want to know. The more I thought about him, the guiltier I felt. But I wasn't going anywhere, and nor was he. We'd have to get used to it, somehow.

I could move on. I'd have to. Nik sure had.

With that intention firmly in mind, I headed toward Myrony's kitchen. There were a few choice morsels with my name on them.

———

Time passed quicker than I would have liked. Myrony kept me busy chopping veggies, lugging bags of grain, stirring the large pot while she tittered about the kitchen.

All too soon, I heard the reverberating clang of the dinner bell.

It was time.

I wiped my hands and emerged from the kitchen, surprised to find the square had been set up with rows of makeshift tables and benches. Flickering Dragonfire lanterns on staffs lined the eating area, and there was already a line forming at Myrony's cook pot.

My gaze swept over the crowd, looking for Nik. He was

nowhere to be found. All the better, I grumbled in the back of my mind. Probably good to give him some space, anyway.

I nearly lost my footing when a small girl brushed past me, pigtails flying out behind her. My eyes widened when I caught a familiar scent. Nik's scent. Another scan of the crowd. He wasn't here.

Then a sick and horrible feeling dawned on me. That little girl...she couldn't be *his*, could she?

My feet stayed rooted to the spot, torn between running to Nik's or running back home. Don't worry about it, I tried to reassure myself. Get your dinner and turn in early. It's been a long day.

That it had, but I couldn't keep my eyes off of her. She had a wild, feral light to her eyes and the way she held herself reminded me of Nik. Then again, everything reminded me of Nik.

It wasn't until one of the villagers in the queue stopped her that my heart burst into double time.

"Hey there, sweetheart. Where's your daddy?"

She looked up at the woman with wide eyes. Kari wore soldier's garb and a sword strapped to her side, but she gazed upon the child kindly, like a mother might.

"He's not coming," the girl mumbled, staring at her feet.

"Why not?" Kari asked. "Is he sick?"

"No," she responded.

Kari put her hands on her hips and looked around the crowd. Finally she took the girls hand and led her toward the food. "Here, let's get you some food. Then we'll find your parents. Okay?"

She nodded silently.

"What's your name, dear?" Kari asked, handing her a plate and spoon.

"Lyria."

I couldn't help but watch. Couldn't help but hear. And then she said those damning words.

"And what's your daddy's name? Does he know you're here?"

"Nik said he wasn't hungry."

The words froze my blood cold. Nik. Oh Goddess, she *was* his! A flare of emotion surged through me and I nearly shifted on the spot, fire flashing through my pores in hot, raging anger.

Good job, Nik! Nice of you to tell me!

I ground my teeth, drawing in a shaky breath through my nose. Sparks burned on my tongue and I tasted ash. Nik had made no mention of her when I came calling. I hadn't seen her, hadn't known she existed. I didn't even know if she was mine.

The thought made my head spin even more, and I sunk down onto one of the nearby benches. Nikolas had a child. And he didn't even tell me. I thought he was dead, for Goddess's sake! And now this?

One thing was for certain as the bustle of people crushed around me. I wasn't hungry anymore.

6

___

NIKOLAS

When the engineers came to remove the enchantments on the house, I thought it would feel different than it did. Like I would feel some sense of freedom, some sense of relief.

None came.

Even as the door opened freely in my hand and the world stretched out beyond, I couldn't bring myself to cross the threshold. Call it whatever you like, but I couldn't shake the feeling that the people out there weren't my friends.

They were my betrayers.

And I wasn't sure I'd survive another confrontation with my mate.

Lyria tugged at my sleeve, begging to go to the square. She was hungry and tired of the rations the Paradox gave us. That much I knew.

So when the dinner bell rang, she took off like a bolt. Out of my grasp and out of the house.

I watched with terror as she fled, pigtails flying out behind her in the wind.

She looked so happy.

She could finally live freely.

The thought shook me out of my stupor and I flew out the door after her. Lyria was only four years old, soon to be five, and war-torn Darkvale was no place for an unattended child.

She had quite the head start though, and disappeared behind the buildings before I knew what had hit me.

Alarm bells screeched in my mind; how could I have let her get so far away from me? Who knew what would happen to her out there? Sure, it wasn't as if she'd gotten lost outside the city walls, but rubble was everywhere and construction was in full swing. No telling what she'd get into.

I fled up the hill toward the square, all fear and guilt forgotten. She was my daughter. My charge. And if I couldn't put my feelings aside and put her first, then what kind of parent was I?

I crested the hill, panting. Quite the crowd had gathered in the square for the first Firefang dinner since the reclamation of Darkvale. I'd been invited, of course, but was too wrapped up in my own misery to care. I'd been so blind my own child wandered away from me.

My eyes scanned the crowd for blond pigtails. No sign of them. Then again, the Firefangs were known for their height and Lyria was just a child. She'd be swallowed up by any throng.

Silently cursing myself, I took a breath and ran down the hill toward the square. Surely someone had seen her. They could point me in the right direction.

Please, I whispered to Glendaria. *Let her be okay.*

The Firefangs were feasting, laughing, and drinking when I staggered onto the scene, sweaty hair stuck to my face. Someone had taken up a lute and begun to play, and a circle of men watched with enraptured glances. They clapped, stomped their feet, raised their mugs to the sky.

Still no sign of her.

"Lyria!" I called, my voice hoarse.

The sound mixed with the laughter and singing of the clansmen, lost to the breeze. I stumbled through the crowd, jostling plates of food and drink as I went.

"Lyria!" I called again, looking around frantically.

"Daddy?" I heard the little voice call and whipped my head around.

There she was, running toward me with outstretched arms. "Daddy!"

I took her into my arms, holding her close at eye level. "Thank the Goddess you're all right. Don't you ever do that again!" My voice shook as relief and the pent up fear spilled out of me.

Her lip quivered.

I sighed. "I'm so sorry, sweetheart." I held her to my chest and she wrapped her arms around me, smearing a snotty nose on my sleeve as she went.

Footsteps kicked up dust on the path. Well-worn combat boots walked toward me. I didn't have to look up to see who they belonged to.

"So this little munchkin's yours." It wasn't a question.

I straightened, still holding Lyria close.

"Yes, she is. Don't you remember what happened that night?"

Marlowe's face blanched. "She's..."

"Yours, yeah. But I'll be damned if you think you're gonna bring all your war and battle with you. She's just a kid. She needs a safe environment to grow up in."

"She needs her other father," Marlowe demanded, taking a step closer.

Lyria blinked up at me, concerned. I soothed her and petted her hair, still holding her to me as if I was afraid she'd fly away.

"This isn't the time or place." I said through gritted teeth. My eyes flitted to the still-largely-oblivious crowd, but if this kept up we'd be the center of attention in no time.

Marlowe crossed his arms and stood straighter, puffing out his chest. The full weight of his alpha pheromones wafted over me, heightening my senses and rousing the dragon within. Ever since he'd presented as alpha when we were children, it was his favorite dirty trick. He knew I couldn't resist him on a primal level. "Let's make it the time and place, then. I'll grab a plate of food for us, we'll go back to my quarters. Talk things out. Deal?"

I swallowed, looking from Lyria to Marlowe and back. Grief and apprehension still gripped me with equal measure, but I wanted to believe that things could be different. For Lyria's sake.

Marlowe was right about one thing, at least: the girl deserved to know her alpha father.

"Okay," I let out a breath. "Fine. Lead the way."

———

The quarters that Marlowe had taken up after returning to Darkvale were much nicer than mine. I guess that came as no surprise—he was alpha, and a commander. What was I but a puny omega left behind?

Well, nicer wasn't quite the word. More central, maybe.

Oh, and not magically reinforced to suppress my shift or prevent my escape. There was that.

The red and gold banners of the Firefangs hung from the walls and a small hammock hung precariously in a corner.

"You sleep in a hammock?" I asked with a grin. Always seemed uncomfortable to me.

Marlowe shrugged as he placed the food down on the small table. "It's what I got used to out in the field. Can't really sleep in a proper bed anymore."

I huffed in amusement. He was still stubborn as ever.

"Now sit, eat. Let's talk."

Lyria gave me a wary glance and I squeezed her hand, nodding. We sat across the table from my former mate. The father of my child.

In the moment, though, my stomach growled painfully. I'd been so busy hurting that I hadn't noticed my hunger. Now that I saw the food in front of us, my mouth watered at the sight.

A big bowl of broth, two small loaves of bread, three apples, a bunch of grapes, and a skinned fish lay on the platter, along with a few cherry tomatoes.

My daughter gazed at the food, then at me, as if looking for permission. "Go on, dig in," I urged her. "You're the hungry one."

She picked at a few of the grapes, eyes alight as they exploded on her tongue. She grabbed more, and then moved onto the bread, shoving it into her mouth as fast as she could.

"Careful now," Marlowe chuckled, watching her. "Don't make yourself sick."

"She's not had real food for quite some time," I glared across the table, my eyes hard. "Let her enjoy herself this once."

"All the more reason to be careful."

I held my gaze.

Marlowe clamped his lips shut and focused on his broth.

We ate in near total silence. Only the call of a bird overhead and the rumbling of the crowd carried over in the wind. That, and the sounds of silverware, plates, and food.

When the platter was empty and my glass drained I leveled my gaze at Marlowe again. Now that the initial shock had passed, I could see him a bit more clearly. He looked different, yes, but not terribly so. He was still handsome. There was no denying that.

His face had grown hard over the years. Harder even than before, and I hadn't known that was possible. I supposed that was one of the reasons I fell for him, though. I'd known him since we were kids, and I was one of the only people that knew him well enough to see beyond that brash exterior.

Underneath it all had been a caring, passionate, and dedicated mate. I wondered if that man was still in there.

Marlowe caught me looking and his face quirked up in a smile.

"Lyria," I said, placing my hand over hers. Her face showed nothing but confusion for a few moments before the pieces fit together. Lyria's mouth hung open, a bread crumb still dangling there.

"This is Marlowe. He and I go way back, don't we?" I eyed him meaningfully.

"Hey there," Marlowe grinned at Lyria. "I knew your dad way back when. I'm sorry I never got to meet you when..."

"What he means to say," I interrupted, squeezing Lyria's hand. "Is that he was gone for a very long time, but he's back now. He wants to be part of our family again."

Lyria sipped at her drink silently, eyes flitting from Marlowe to me. I wondered how much of this she understood. It was a complex topic for anyone to wrap their head around, much less a four-year-old.

My chest tightened as I waited for her reaction.

"Can I have more grapes?" she asked, ignoring the topic entirely.

Marlowe and I looked at one another and snorted with laughter. A grin broke across his face just as it did across mine. In that moment, I almost remembered the way things used to be. Why I'd fallen in love with him in the first place.

"What?" Lyria whined, looking up at me.

I took her hand. "Let's go get you your grapes, sweetheart."

She brightened at that, and I led her back out into the gathering.

————

A pile of fruit later, Lyria was looking sated and rather sleepy. She yawned and tugged on my shirt, pointing toward the west. Toward home.

"Looks like it's just about bedtime," Marlowe noted. "I'd be happy to walk you back home, or she can take a nap in the hammock if she wants..." he trailed off, as if thinking better of it.

"Thank you, but we really should get going. Come on, Lyria."

I looked over to her. She slumped over the table with her mouth open slightly, breaths coming in a slow, easy rhythm.

Marlowe grabbed my hand suddenly. The electric

sparkles of chemistry I'd long since forgotten crackled across my skin just as powerfully as they had our first night together. I snapped my gaze up to his, where his dragon irises burned bright.

"Stay," he urged me. "A little longer. Please."

I froze, considering the options. I had no intention of going down this path with him again. At least, my rational mind didn't. It knew how badly I'd been hurt last time, and wanted to keep me from feeling that ever again.

My heart and my dragon, however, had other ideas.

I opened my mouth, then shut it, grasping for the words.

"We've got a lot of catching up to do." Marlowe ran a hand through his hair and stared at the ground. "I'm..." he gulped visibly. "I'm sorry, Nik. I am. I spent the last five years wishing I could change the past, but I can't, and it's killing me."

"You had no idea what it was like," I started, my voice a broken whisper. "Raising a daughter alone...being treated like a slave..."

He squeezed my hand. "Then tell me. I have all night. Here, let's help Lyria into bed."

As gently as possible, we helped Lyria to the hammock, who cradled herself into it easily. She woke and mumbled a bit, but I gave her a soothing smile and brushed the hair from her face. Poor thing was exhausted. Lyria yawned and fell back into an easy, peaceful sleep.

"She's beautiful," Marlowe said, not looking away from the hammock. "If I had only known…"

I gave him a grim smile, placing a hand on his shoulder. "There are things that both of us could have done better."

Marlowe covered my hand with his own, squeezing and rubbing the stubble of his cheek against me. "We were at war. Every day, hardly sleeping, never knowing if the next day would be my last…" His eyes widened and he grimaced. "Never knowing what happened to you."

"I'm glad you came back to me," I whispered before I could stop myself. I leaned my head against his chest and listened to the steady thump thump thump of his heart there. This was the Marlowe I remembered.

Marlowe ran a hand through my long blond hair and kissed the top of my head, holding me close. "I told you I would. I'll always come back for you, Nikolas. And I'm just sorry it took me so long."

We stayed like that for what seemed like ages, and the cobwebs of time fell away piece by piece. The road back to being mates wasn't an easy one, and I didn't pretend that it would be. But we'd taken the first step, and that meant everything to me.

7

MARLOWE

We spent the night talking, sipping the wine I'd found in the cellar, talking and reminiscing about times past. It was a weird sort of duality.

One the one hand, here was this man, this mate that I had known my whole life. Who meant everything to me and who knew me better than anyone. Or at least, had at one time.

But there was a novelty to it all. The way my skin tingled when we touched, the way my heart leapt when he smiled at me, it was like first date jitters all over again.

Things were different now. That much was for sure. But now I had something worth fighting for.

Our little girl snored in the hammock and rolled over sleepily, mouth hanging open. The surge of pride and longing that washed over me was startling. My child. My daughter. My baby.

Ours.

I couldn't imagine what it must have been like for Nikolas to raise her alone, not knowing if I'd ever return. Not to mention the living conditions they'd forced him into. Living essentially behind bars for years on end, never able to shift or join the outside world? My dragon rumbled with rage at the unfairness of it all. I wanted someone's head for this. I wanted blood.

But we'd already defeated the main Paradox forces. We were safe now. We were home.

That didn't stop the righteous anger from burning me inside out. I didn't know how yet, but I was going to make this up to him. I had to make up for all those years I couldn't be around. I needed to be the mate, the alpha, and the father my family needed. Now more than ever.

The moon had reached its zenith when a knock came at the door. I glanced at Nik over the wine glasses and put the goblet down carefully, listening.

The knock came again.

A cold shiver passed through me from head to foot as I stood and stared at the door.

Someone was out there, and I wasn't expecting any visitors.

"Who goes there?" I called, trying to keep my voice low. I didn't want to scare Lyria.

"Urgent message from the scouts, sir. You're needed at the council hall immediately."

I blew out a breath through my nose and pale tendrils of smoke rose toward the ceiling.

I looked back to Nik, who wore an expression of weary resignation. "Go on," he waved me off. "Do your thing."

I stepped forward and placed a hand on his shoulder. "I'll come back. I will. That's a promise." I bent down and pecked a kiss on his forehead, then grabbed my cloak and rushed out the door.

This time, I wouldn't leave him stranded.

I followed the runner to the council hall where all the officers had already gathered. Guess I had a habit of running late.

"What's all this about?" I said, yawning and stretching. "Have you any idea what time it is?"

"We do," Rayn said. "That's why we called you here."

Two men marched into the clan hall, dragging a tall gangly man by the shoulders. His arms were in shackles, a black mask obscuring his mouth.

"We found the Sorcerer," Eron said, pushing the man to his knees. "We caught him skulking about outside. He knows something, I'm sure of it."

I smelled the ashy crackle of dragon fire and held out a hand to stop it. "He's more use to us alive." I paced around the man, noting his long tattered robes, his gaunt face, the way his eyes darted to and fro. Sorcerers were known to nullify the powers of dragon shifters, but with the proper precautions their talents could be subdued.

The mask covered his mouth so he could not form incantations, and the shackles were laced with a subtle poison that disrupted their magical auras. How they'd gotten hold of such a poison was beyond me; they must have found it when ransacking the Paradox's stores.

There was a reason that the Sorcerers were so dangerous. The poison and the ritual to imbue it was a dark, forbidden magic.

Just what had the Cogs been into here?

"Let him speak, but keep the shackles on 'im." I commanded, and Eron ripped the mask away. The Sorcerer gasped in a clean breath, still struggling against his restraints. He bared his ugly teeth at me, railing against his captors. They held firm. He wasn't going anywhere.

"Tell me your name, Sorcerer." I folded my hands, staring over them at the man in front of me. A tiny disruption vibrated through the air, but it wasn't enough to dull my powers. I could roast him right here if I had to.

The man stared at the ground, refusing to meet my gaze.

"You'll make it easier on yourself if you cooperate," I said evenly.

Seconds passed. The only sounds were the Sorcerer's labored breathing.

"Elias," he said finally.

"And is that your real name?" I cocked an eyebrow.

"Yes." He still didn't look at me.

I paced around to his side, admiring the handiwork of the shackles that kept him subdued. They shimmered with a sickly green light. Better him than me.

"Now tell me, Elias. What were you doing in my clan's territory? Were you hired by someone, or did you happen upon our land by coincidence?"

"Why would I tell you?" Long tendrils of shaggy hair hung down over his forehead. The strained years of seclusion had not done the ailing Sorcerer race any favors.

"We can help each other, I believe. You tell me what you've seen on your travels, and in return, I offer you the comfort of my home. You shall share our hearth in return for your loyalty. But be assured, Elias, betray that trust and you will burn in fires the like of which you've never imagined."

Elias raised his chin at long last, meeting my eyes. His gaze was a startling blue, clear and almost crystalline.

"We can work out a relationship that benefits the both of us. I am sure of it." I clipped off the last several words and sunk into a chair, staring at him at eye level.

He held my gaze, unflinching. Here was a man who knew how to hold his own. "You'd never believe me if I told you," Elias growled.

"Oh really? Try me, boy. I've seen rather a lot of unbelievable things recently." My lips turned up in an intimidating grin.

Elias snarled and a momentary disruption floated through the air again. He yanked at his bonds, teeth flashing in the light.

"Replace the mask," I said, waving him away. "Hold him until he's ready to talk."

The two officers wrestled the mask back over his face, the Sorcerer's eyes wide with alarm.

"I've got all the time in the world, Elias. But you don't." I gave him a last cold-hearted glare and turned my back to him. "Take him away."

Screams. Shouts. Then a thump, and the sound of a body dragging across the floor.

The door closed behind me and I sighed, rubbing my temples. I had no time for this. I needed to be with Nik.

But I needed to be here for my clan as well. Last time I'd made the wrong choice. Would I make it again?

I looked to the other clan members gathered in the hall. "I want double the guard presence, and if we so much as smell a Sorcerer nearby, you come to me first, understand?"

The men nodded.

"And what of Elias?"

"He will talk soon enough. Their kind are a selfish people. All we need to do is show him we're better than the other option. Do keep an eye on him, though. I don't want any...mishaps." I shivered to think what havoc a rogue Sorcerer could wreak on our recovering clan.

"As you wish, Commander."

"Any news on the Paradox? I'm not naive enough to think we've wiped them out for good."

"No sign of them as of yet, but perhaps the Sorcerer knows something. We'll keep an eye on him."

My mouth twisted into a scowl. The Sorcerers had a bloody reputation. Kidnapping the Clan Alpha's mate, pulling him away from battle at the eleventh hour...even if we could get Elias on our side, a Sorcerer was never to be trusted.

8

NIKOLAS

Reintegrating into clan life was going to be a challenge. Thank the Goddess I had my little Lyria to keep me on my toes.

In the past few days, the Firefangs had returned to claim Darkvale, Lucien had arrived with half a human village in tow, and the remaining residences were way, way too crowded.

No doubt about it—things were gonna be different around here.

I waited in Marlowe's hideout, sipping at his wine and thinking about the future. The moon rose and fell in the sky. The wine disappeared. Lyria sniffed and shifted in the hammock, but never woke completely. Poor thing, she was exhausted.

Sleep began to tug at my eyelids as well. I blinked and

shook my head, willing myself awake. I didn't want to leave. Not yet. Marlowe said he'd come back.

And I desperately wanted to believe him.

I knew he had duties as commander. I knew that our peace was still fragile. But it hurt, seeing him go like that. Would this one night of connection be all I got this time?

I stewed in my thoughts as my stomach clenched and unclenched. I never should have let my guard down. Not even for her.

My eyelids drooped again, and darkness fell over me like a blanket.

Movement behind me jolted me awake. My heart squeezed in fear, jumping into double-time. I whirled around.

Oh. It was him.

He was back.

"Marlowe," I mumbled, my voice hoarse from sleep. "What time is it?"

"Late," he answered. "Didn't know you'd still be here. How's Lyria?" Marlowe stepped over to the hammock and eyed the sleeping girl. His face softened, the lines of stress fading away. "She's a gem, isn't she?" His voice was soft, almost a whisper.

Pride lit up my face. "She is." He couldn't change the subject completely, though. "What was all that about?"

My heart still thrummed in my rib cage, the familiar tendrils of panic clawing their way through my gut. After five years in captivity, I wasn't sure I knew what safety felt like anymore.

"You sure she won't wake?" Marlowe asked, tilting a head at the hammock.

I moved to stand beside my mate. He smelled delicious, even with the undercurrent of fear vibrating through the air. I looked up at him and placed a hand on his shoulder. "She sleeps like a rock. Come on, sit down. You can talk to me."

We faced off, Marlowe's stoic expression waging war against my concerned one. Eventually, I won out. He let out a breath and stepped around me, sinking onto the bench at the table. "Wine's gone," he noted, looking at the bottle. "Someone's been busy." Marlowe let out a little laugh, raising an eyebrow at me.

"I was thirsty," I retorted with my hands on my hips. That, and I didn't know how else to deal with the sudden emotion flooding my body and soul.

After all these years, Marlowe was back. And he wanted to be there for our daughter.

But could it be that easy?

My head still swum with the alcohol, but I was clear-headed enough to take a seat and level my gaze at him.

"We're still at war, aren't we." It wasn't a question. The

words rang out with all the finality of a death knell. For people like Marlowe, the fight was never over.

Marlowe chewed his lip for a moment in thought, then gave a curt nod. He leaned forward to wrap his arms around me. His breath was warm on my neck, tickling the skin there into gooseflesh. His scent drove my dragon wild, pushing against my skin, desperate to be one with him as we had in the past.

He was so close.

"Perhaps there are things more important than war," Marlowe rumbled into my ear. A shiver vibrated down my spine all the way to my cock, which grew with each passing second. "Like family."

The word echoed through the small room, filling me with a hope I hadn't had in five long years. *Family.*

"You mean it?" I asked, turning my head to match his gaze. His fiery pupils dilated and held me rapt.

"You know I do," he replied. "Your dragon knows, deep down. But will you believe it?"

I shivered again, even though there was no draft. The feeling went all the way down to my soul, to the depths of my dragon I'd kept at bay for so long. In its place roared a fire I'd all but forgotten. A fire for him.

"Let me prove myself to you." Marlowe's lips caressed the tender skin at my ear, moving down to my neck right where the omega pheromones were strongest. He took in a large whiff, groaning almost in pain. "I've missed that so much."

Before I could stop myself, I said, "I missed you."

"Let us fly again as we once did." Marlowe squeezed my hands in his own, taunting my dragon further. "Let us take to the skies, just the two of us."

Visions of cool, fresh air, stars, and clouds flashed through my mind. The feeling of pushing off the ground, of gliding on the air currents, of flapping my wings and finally getting to stretch—

"I can't." I drew away, shaking my head. "I've got a kid to look after now."

"And I bet you've never taken her to the skies either." Marlowe's voice took on a note of concern. "Our kind aren't meant to stay here on the ground. Suppressing your true nature like that...it's not healthy."

I recoiled. Now he was trying to tell me how to raise my kid? The thought stung.

"So you're the parenting expert now?" The bitterness of my words poisoned the lust I'd felt only moments before. "They *poisoned* me, Mar! They cursed that damn house so I couldn't shift! I couldn't get out, I couldn't use my powers, I couldn't escape..."

Marlowe's face crumpled. "Let me help you," he said at last, reaching out a hand.

"I don't need your help," I snapped with more venom in my voice than I intended. "We survived without your help for five years, Mar. Five long, hard years under Paradox control. Do you have any idea what that was like for me? For her?"

Marlowe's face crumpled. "No, but—"

"Daddy?" Lyria's tired voice snapped me out of my rage instantly. We both glanced over at the far side of the room where she'd woke and sat up, staring at both of us.

Shit, I cursed under my breath. *How much of that did she see?*

I swallowed the anger and hurt down deep, the same way I did every day that Marlowe was gone. I plastered on my father face and gave Lyria a smile that didn't quite reach my eyes.

"Hey there, darling. Have a good sleep?"

She blinked and yawned. "Yeah." She paused a moment, her lip wobbling. Then, "Why were you shouting?"

Her eyes were so full, so innocent. Guilt and shame hit me like a one-two punch straight to the heart.

"Lyria," I soothed. "Let's go home, hmm? I'll grab an extra tray of snacks for us. My treat."

She frowned at me with disbelieving eyes. I let out a sigh as the weight sunk deeper in my chest.

I took her small hand and helped her out of the

hammock. She was still wobbly from sleep and clung to my pant leg. "Bye," she waved at Marlowe as I led her away.

Some timing, sweetheart, I thought wearily as we stepped out into the rising sun.

9

_____

NIKOLAS

Days passed and I saw no hide nor hair of Marlowe. It was just as well. I could take care of my girl by myself. Always had.

He barely even knew her, or what we'd been through together. A strain of worry squeezed itself through my veins. Did he even know *me* anymore?

I left the house more and more often, venturing out with Lyria to the kitchens or simply to reacquaint myself with the streets that had once been home.

Things hadn't changed so much, in some ways. In others, they were irrevocably different. The stone structures were the same. The buildings and the roads led to the same places. Many of the people I'd known from back in the day. But they were different now.

So we all were.

Marlowe used to tell me that war changed a person. I never really knew what that meant until I saw it on their faces.

People moved with the determined, purposeful gait of one on a mission. They didn't hang back to talk with the neighbors or smile at passing children. Life in exile had forced them into strict regiment and routine. They were all like *him* now.

I grimaced at the bitter taste in my mouth. He'd come back, hadn't he? And they *did* manage to rout the Paradox from our walls.

It didn't matter. The machinations of politics meant nothing to me. The Iron Paradox was gone and the Firefangs ruled once more. That was enough.

It had to be.

I'd begun taking Lyria to interact with the other kids in the village. Thomas was starting a school for both human and dragons alike to learn and grow. It was quite the progressive concept, given that many human villages still loathed and feared dragonkind.

But that was another way that the Clan Alpha's new mate had surprised us all. When Lucien returned with a human mate in tow, I had to admit I was confused. Lucien had loved Caldo fiercely. Anyone could have seen that. But in that night of fire and death, Caldo had met a fate even worse than I had. He lay there, begging for his life, as he bled out onto the sands and they dragged me away.

Death was part of life, but to see it so cruelly taken? It turned my stomach sour. The oncoming morning sickness probably had something to do with it, too, in retrospect.

Lyria was spending the day with another of the shifter girls in the village when I decided to go see my old friend Lucien. He'd helped me once before. He was the one that helped me win Marlowe's heart in the first place. Surely, he'd know what to do.

The Clan Alpha's quarters looked much as I'd remembered them, only there were quite a few more people living there now. Lucien's human mate, Alec, had brought along his family from their village of Steamshire, and until new residences could be completed they were staying in the Alpha's quarters.

I opened the door to see a boy run past, tailed quickly by another boy chasing him. An aging woman sat by the fireplace, the clack-clack-clack of knitting needles a steady rhythm.

Ducking out of the way of their game with a smile, I crossed the threshold. Lucien looked up to see the visitor and grinned widely as he recognized me.

"Nikolas Lastir!" He boomed, clapping me on the back in an aggressive hug/chest-bump combo. "Goddess, it's good to see you. We'd thought you were dead."

I offered him a half-smile. I didn't come here to talk about my captivity. But everyone kept bringing it up.

"Listen, I just want to personally apologize, Nik. Had I known..." Lucien's voice trailed off and his forehead creased in concern.

"I'm fine," I brushed it off, though in my mind I was anything but. "I wanted to talk to you about something."

A spark of mischief glinted in his eye. "Just like old times?"

I had to give him a little smile at that. It seemed like so long ago now that I'd come to seek his counsel. Marlowe and I were nothing but childhood friends back then.

"Something like that," I said and took a seat.

"How's Marlowe, anyway? Is he..." Lucien cleared his throat. "Taking it okay? I haven't spoken to him much since the debriefing."

I gave a rueful chuckle. "That's what I wanted to talk to you about."

Lucien slid a platter of biscuits across the table. Their fluffy golden tops still steamed. "Go on, they're delicious."

I tried to politely decline, but Lucien pushed the plate closer. "I demand it. You've got to try one. Tell him, Alec. Aren't they heavenly?"

We'd caught him in the middle of a bite and he nodded

with a mouth full of food. After a moment he swallowed and added, "It's like a party in your mouth!"

We had a good laugh at that. The children ran and played, the woman clack-clack-clacked, and things were almost normal again.

Almost.

"Fine," I rolled my eyes and reached for the plate. "I'll try one of these magical biscuits. But I won't promise I'll like it." I stuck out my lip in a pout then took a tentative bite.

Flavors exploded on my tongue in an instant. Warm, flaky bread combined with a rich, buttery flavor and something else I couldn't name. I nearly moaned as I popped another bite into my mouth before noticing the snickering faces in front of me.

I cleared my throat and placed it down on the plate, swiping a few crumbs away from my lips. "They are..." I said with a blush, "Quite good. Never had anything like it."

The men erupted into laughter and I couldn't hold mine in any longer.

Lucien threw an arm around Alec's shoulder and gave it a squeeze. "You have Alec's clan to thank for that." He pointed at the biscuit. "That's a human recipe. Incredible what they can do with food, isn't it?"

"Yeah," I agreed before scarfing down the rest of the

biscuit. "I hope there's more where that came from." I grinned at Alec. "Are all your people such good cooks?"

Alec shook his head with an amused grin. "Only some of them."

"Now what's this about, Nik?" Lucien returned his gaze to me, propping his chin on his hands. "Trouble in paradise?"

I groaned and rolled my eyes. It was true, though. "You could say that. I just...I'm not sure what to do now that he's back. We were so close, and that night I thought I lost him forever."

Lucien closed his eyes and nodded. "I remember it well." Alec squeezed his hand. I hadn't been the only one to lose someone they loved that night.

"I thought we were gonna be together forever. Through anything. But he never came back. I couldn't find him, couldn't reach him on the Link. And as Darkvale burned they dragged me away."

Lucien's eyes opened again and he gave me a tired smile. "I offer you only my sincerest condolences. In all our time in the field, I never knew they would stoop that low. We'd been told that the city was cleared of Firefangs. That there were no survivors. I can admit now that we were wrong."

No survivors. The thought sizzled on my skin like water on a hot pan. Is that why he never returned?

"You were able to overcome the Curse of the Dragonheart, clearly." I shifted in my seat and gestured to Alec. "But it doesn't appear Marlowe was ever afflicted. Why is that?"

The deepest fears in my heart told me that it was because he'd never loved me to begin with, that he could not break a heart he had not given to another. I feared it, with every fiber of my being. But what other reason could there be?

"Marlowe...well, you know how he is. I can assure you that he was quite affected by your disappearance, even though he may not show it."

"He was?" My voice was quiet to my ears.

"Marlowe is a man of action. Of black and white. Of problems and solutions. The problem came up that his mate, his lover, was missing. Instead of wallowing in the pain, he simply forced it away, bottled it up. You wouldn't think it at first glance, but I've been living and fighting with him in close proximity for half a decade. You learn things about one another no one knows. And let me tell you, Nik. It's eating him from the inside out."

I blinked at him, digesting the words.

From the inside out...

"I have a daughter, too." I blurted the words out.

Lucien's eyes widened for only a moment. "A secret baby...that does make things difficult."

CONNOR CROWE

"She's his!" My voice rose.

"Let me handle this one." Alec nudged Lucien and considered me. "Alphas can be like bricks sometimes," He offered with a grin. "Marlowe especially. But it sounds like he wants to make things right. He won't come 'round if you're all laggy about it though. Remember, you need to let him think it was all his idea in the first place. Even if it totally wasn't." Alec gave me a wink and Lucien sputtered.

"Hey!"

They cut off into flirtatious teasing as I turned over Alec's words in my mind. He had a point. Perhaps I was letting my grief cloud my judgement.

And after smelling him again for the first time in half a decade, my dragon wanted, no, needed, more.

"Being a parent is tough stuff," Alec agreed, ducking Lucien's playful swats. "I learned that fast. Still learning. Couldn't imagine going it alone like you did. But you know what that tells me?"

"What?"

"That you're strong enough, wise enough, and totally badass enough to win him back. If you run back to his place now, you can catch him before the council meeting...I'm sure no one will notice if he's a bit late." Alec gave me that knowing wink again.

"Hey, I will!" Lucien clamored, but with a good-natured grin.

I glanced out the window at the sun. It was barely midday, and Lyria would be on her playdate for another few hours.

I had an idea.

"Go on, go get him." Alec shooed me from the room. "And remember, the secret to any alpha's heart is food!"

"Thanks," I said to both of them with a chuckle, bowing my head in gratitude.

"It's not totally selfless, you know," Lucien called from behind me. I threw on my cloak and was already halfway to the door. "Tell Marlowe to get that stick out of his ass! I want my friend back too."

I considered that mental image, amused, and rushed off across town.

10

MARLOWE

If fucking-things-up was an Olympic sport, I'd take home the gold. No question.

Days passed to bleary routine as I threw myself into my duties. I made the rounds, sat in on every boring meeting with the scouts, even helped the schoolmaster Thomas wrangle children. I had motives other than pure altruism, sure. I thought I'd catch another glimpse of Lyria, but she wasn't there.

It kept my hands busy. It kept me moving.

That was what mattered, right?

I hadn't dared return to Nik's place. My dragon had been ready to pounce. The magical energy had reverberated between us, pulled taut like a perfect lute string.

And then I opened my big mouth.

With a dissonant twang, there went the string. There went the connection. Gone.

So deep in my thoughts was I that I barely noticed the knock at the door. It came again before I fully registered.

"Oh, who it it now?" I mumbled and rubbed my forehead. I had mistakenly thought that perhaps I'd get some alone time once we returned to Darkvale. But it seemed like the requests came in even more furiously. There were things to repair, to rebuild, to restore. And somehow that fell to me.

I glanced at the simple clock on the wall, heralding the arrival of midday. That meant there was only an hour till the next meeting, and I'd intended to use that time to relax.

The knock came again.

"What is it?" I growled irritably. "It can wait till the meeting!"

Silence.

Then—"It's me."

I'd know that voice anywhere.

"Nik?" I asked, my voice faint.

"Yeah. Open up."

Why of all times had he chose to visit now? He clearly was upset with me, and yet...

A rumbling of fire coursed through my chest as I heard the words in my mind. A faint echo at first, like a voice reaching through thick mist.

Come on, Mar. I know you're in there.

I froze. I'd closed off any connection I had to my mate and our Link long ago, to keep from hurting further. And yet there it was. He'd reached past those walls, for the briefest of moments. Now there was no doubt in my mind about his sincerity.

I can hear you. Come on.

My mouth hung open as I moved toward the door. I took a deep breath, ran a hand through my hair, and slid the latch.

Nik stood on the other side, hands in his pockets but with a desperate fire in his eyes. One I'd only seen once before, when I'd so foolishly challenged him to a duel.

I'd felt stupid then. But even stupider now.

"C'mere, you idiot." Nikolas stepped over the threshold and threw himself at me, wrapping his arms around my neck in a hug.

I stood motionless, not daring to believe. His heady scent invaded my nose. I groaned and lost myself in the scent, rousing not only my dragon but also my cock.

"I'm sorry," Nik breathed as he captured my lips. "I'm here now."

It didn't take long for my dragon to catch up and I held him closer, pressing his heated skin to mine.

Oh, Goddess. Was he in heat? Was that what this was about?

Nik locked eyes with mine. "Heat would imply I'm looking for just any alpha." He kissed me again, slow and deep. "But I'm not."

"And what are you looking for?" My voice quivered. I wanted to praise whatever had brought about this change of heart, but it was too sudden. Too strange.

"We need to talk," Nik said, pulling at my shirt buttons.

I laughed incredulously. "This doesn't look like talking to me."

"I can multitask." He finished the buttons and pulled my shirt away, leaving my chest on full display for him. My brain was still racing to keep up, still echoing with alarm bells, but the feeling of his hands on my skin muted out those worries.

"I thought you were dead. Hated it. Hated myself. Hated you. And then I had her, and hell, Marlowe, I don't know anything about kids—"

"Looks like you did an okay job. She's beautiful." I rubbed little circles on his back, suddenly desperate for more. Taking my turn, I slid my hands under his shirt and lifted it over his head until we stood there, bare chested and face-to-face.

"I want this to work, Mar." Nik's voice cracked as he stared deep into my eyes. A man could lose himself in those fiery orbs. I certainly had. "Lyria needs a family. Two dads. Love. Learning. Opportunity. And she can't have that if you leave me again."

I winced.

"Promise me, Mar." He nuzzled my neck, moving down to the collarbone and planting a line of kisses there. My head spun, but I was still rational enough to process Nik's words. "Promise me, for her."

I breathed in his scent, roaming my hands down the heated flesh there. Warring emotions battled inside me. I was a commander. A fighter. That was my identity, who I'd always been. I couldn't just give that up. But I couldn't lose Nik again either. I remembered again the reason I fought. I wasn't just some bloodthirsty barbarian. I was a protector. Of myself. My people. My family.

My daughter.

The words spilled out of me. "I love you more than life itself. You should know that. Always have. Always did. I'm...not too good at handling emotional stuff. When we left, when all was lost, I..." I brushed a nervous hand across my hair again. "Goddess, I thought you were gone for good. I tried to get back to you. But it all came down around us and next thing I knew, you were gone, and off we went. I did what I had to do for our clan, but damned if I don't regret that decision every day."

I pulled away to get a good look at his face. His eyes were half-lidded with desire, the other half shining with emotion. The tingling connection ignited between us once more. Our relationship had been a ripped fabric for so many years, but finally we could patch that wound. A single thread of soul-bound magic moved through my heart, my arms, my eyes. It pushed out through my fingertips and crackled wherever we touched like an electric shock. Slowly but surely, this ripped fabric could become whole again.

"I want to be with you." Nikolas squeezed my hands, his eyes all liquid amber. "Not just for her. But for us. We really had something, didn't we?"

I chuckled. "Yeah, we sure did."

"Take two?" Nik mumbled against my lips.

"Take two," I promised, and closed the gap.

———

I gave myself over to instinct, trusting my dragon to lead the way. The clock still ticked ominously in the corner, counting down the seconds until my next meeting. Right now, though? It didn't matter. I had my mate, and we were together again.

"How do you feel about a quickie?" I whispered in his ear, grinning.

"Good," Nik breathed. "The sooner the better. But only if there's more to come later."

I rumbled low in my chest. "There will be much more later. That is a promise."

"Now show me what you're made of, alpha." Nik taunted me, holding his arms out wide. "Come and get it."

I charged. Our bodies met in a resounding crash, the air rushing out of us as we came together. I raked my hands everywhere I could reach—his neck, his abs, his back. They traveled down, toward the waistband of his pants.

Yes, there was that magnificent ass.

"Good to see that's one thing that hasn't changed." I gave it a squeeze and produced a high-pitched yelp from my omega in return. That just made me want to do it more.

"Careful," I warned him with a nip at his neck. "You don't wanna release the dragon, do you?"

"Maybe I do," Nik retorted and his hands were at my pants, unfastening.

I could only growl in response.

"There's no bed," Nikolas said breathlessly.

"No," I agreed with a mischievous quirk of my eyebrow. "But there is a hammock."

"Can we—?"

"Only one way to find out."

I took Nik's hand and led him to the hammock, my heart beating a steady tattoo in my chest. After the long years of silence, of cold nights sleeping alone, it was finally happening. I was back. He wanted me. This time I wouldn't let him down.

"Are you sure it will hold?" Nik asked, eyeing the swaying cotton hammock.

"Shh," I pressed a finger over his lips. My breath came in hot pants, and if alphas could have heat I'd be lost right now. He was here, so hot, so ready. My dragon vibrated with pleasure, with recognition, with magic. "Trust me." The words bounced off the walls and back onto us. It was a near repeat of our first mating. Seemed fitting.

Nik opened his mouth to speak, then pressed his lips shut. He leaned backward, settling into the hammock and throwing his hands over his head. He wove his long fingers into the netting holding the cotton to the stand and gripped tight. Nikolas threw his legs over each side of the hammock, spreading them wide to reveal his wet and ready channel. Even from this vantage point and the dim light I could see the glistening slick calling to me. "Come and get me, alpha." He grinned with a raised eyebrow and I was powerless to resist.

Be gentle, I tried to remind myself as I lowered myself onto the sleeping hammock. Up until now it had been purely utilitarian. My years on the road had given me no time or reason to collect furniture, and I'd gotten used to the relaxed slumber that a hammock brought me. But now there was an omega in my bed. A very wet, very needy omega. And if I wasn't careful, I'd bring the whole thing down on top of us.

I hooked a leg over the side and lowered myself onto Nik as the wooden stand squealed. I froze and waited a moment—it held. With another breath I lowered myself all the way down, onto Nik's bare skin as our groins pressed together in a hot, heady dance. My hips thrusted of their own volition, seeking him out. The hammock swung and bounced, adding momentum to my movements.

Nik grasped the ropes above him and bit his lip, staring off into space. "Fuck, I thought you said this was a quickie."

"It is." I grabbed my throbbing cock in my hand and guided it to his channel, relishing the breathy moans as I pressed against the opening. Goddess, he was wet. My mind was nothing but a haze of lust and fire, the dragon within me roaring and begging for control. "You like that?"

"Yes," Nik gasped. "Please."

With a push, I guided myself in. A groan rumbled out of my throat before I could stop myself and I clamped down on Nik's shoulders, my fingers momentarily lengthening into claws. Nik sucked in a breath and I pushed myself deeper to savor that sweet heat.

The hammock squealed and rocked with each motion of

my hips, the two of us swaying together in time with each thrust. I pressed myself deeper, all the way to the hilt.

"Goddess," I cursed, leaning forward to plant a few kisses down his collarbone. "I missed this."

"I missed you." Nik whispered.

There was no doubt about that any longer.

I bucked and twisted. My motions became more desperate, more ragged. Breath came in quick gasps as I held onto him for leverage, the squeaking of the hammock stand in the background the only anchor to reality.

After all this time, my dragon had not forgotten the scent of his mate. Nor had I.

The connection between us strengthened and closed, linking our minds and souls in a way that only true mates could. In that moment, the brain fog cleared. The walls I'd so carefully erected crumbled down. And there he was. There he always was. Waiting for me.

I eyed the mating bite I'd placed on Nik's neck so long ago. The scar still showed, a shiny white reminder of the past. What if I could do that a second time? What would happen?

I roared and smashed my hips into Nik's. Sweat and pheromones filled the tent and my omega's sounds of pleasure kept me going. "I'm getting close," Nik wailed, using his feet on the floor to push himself up around me even further. Flames crackled in the back of my throat and the sparks danced on my tongue. Battle, violence, blood—they had nothing on this.

My knot began to swell as I felt my balls tighten. I held my breath, freezing for only a moment. There was no turning back now.

"Take me, Mar." Nik pumped upward furiously. "Take me." His eyes rolled back into his head as his dick jerked and spurted gobs of hot nectar across his chest and mine. The scent rose up and smothered me. I was lost.

The dragon pushed forward and I threw my head back, smoke boiling from my nostrils. With superhuman strength I thrusted madly into him and just as I reached my breaking point, so too did the hammock stand. A resounding crack of splintered wood and the sensation of weightlessness gripped me for only a microsecond before Nik and I tumbled to the ground in a heap.

"Fuck you're heavy!" Nik groaned. He held on for dear life as the roller coaster took us higher, higher, higher, then...

"Goddess, Nik!" The world came undone around us in a million sparkling points of light as I thrashed against him and my knot locked us together, panting, in the wreckage.

11

MARLOWE

The afterglow would have to wait.

A glance at the clock sent my heart into overdrive. I dislodged myself as soon as my knot would let me. "Shit, I'm late!"

"Wha?" Nikolas mumbled sleepily, blinking up at me. He was still sprawled out on the floor with that lazy, sated expression. Couldn't blame him.

"The council meeting," I mumbled as I wiped myself down with an errant towel and threw on my uniform. "We've news from the Sorcerer." I cinched the belt around my waist and pulled on my boots.

"The hell are you doing with a Sorcerer?" Nik's eyes went wide.

"Long story," I muttered. "Little bastard was spying on us."

Nik sat up at that. "I'm coming with you." He rolled to his feet, only a little wobbly.

I threw the cloak around my shoulders and looked back at him. His hair stuck out in all directions, his face was sweaty, and he smelled like sex.

Just wait until the council members get a load of this, I snickered to myself.

"You sure about that?" Waiting for Nik would only slow me down, but the fading soul magic that had bound us together urged me to give him another chance. We couldn't be a true family if I kept sticking to my old habits. I stood my ground and waited.

He pulled on a pair of pants and ran a hand through his hair. Nik's hand on my shoulder steadied my racing heart. "We're mates. No more secrets."

No more secrets. What would that even feel like? I didn't know, and didn't have time to figure out.

"Come on. And hurry." I grabbed his hand as he threw on a jacket and we stumbled out into the city.

———

You might as well call being late my brand, by now. When I entered the chamber with Nik in tow, the officers looked up at me with carefully schooled expressions.

"I do hope we weren't interrupting anything,

Commander." Lucien gave me a knowing grin as we entered. I glared daggers at him. The other men didn't dare say a word.

"Not at all," I said in my practiced commander voice. "My mate has some...ideas on how we might subdue the oncoming threat." I squeezed his hand and gave him a warning glance as his eyes widened.

"Very well, then." Tork folded his hands and sat. He gestured at the two seats at the head of the table. "Let's get started."

Nik followed me silently and sat in the strong wooden chair to my right while I took my place at the head.

"What news of the Sorcerer?" I asked, looking around the chamber. "Where is he?"

A moment of silence. Lucien looked to Andreas, our intelligence officer. "He's on his way back as we speak." Andreas said, furrowing his brow. He placed a hand to his temple as if with a headache.

"You sent him into the field without my knowledge?" Sparks burned on my tongue as I turned my ire on Andreas. "What if he betrays us?"

Andreas did not so much as flinch. "He's not alone. We've sent guards along with him and we'll know if anything goes awry. If his information proves true, we'll keep him. If he's lying, he'll die. Simple as that."

I leaned back in my chair and folded my hands,

grumbling low in my chest. I didn't like that they were doing things behind my back. What else had I missed out on?

"Anything else you've been loath to tell me?" I asked, trying to keep the venom from my voice.

"Nothing else, Commander." Andreas lowered his gaze.

A knock at the door cut through the tension in the room as we looked to see the visitor.

"Who goes there?" Lucien called out. "This meeting is for Firefang Council members only."

"We've returned with the Sorcerer. He speaks the truth." The voice came muffled through the thick iron-banded door, but audible enough.

"Let him in," Lucien waved a hand, and the guards at the door drew the latch. Two men in Firefang garb led another man in shackles through the door, and not gently either. One of the men I recognized as Kaine Maxwell. He was joined by his cousin Ward. Despite Kaine's age he was as strong and quick as any of our young alphas.

The captive's hands and feet were bound with glowing chains, the ankle shackles only far enough apart to take stumbling steps. No running away for this one.

The man's face was drawn and gaunt with age, but his eyes burned when they recognized me all the same.

"Elias," I said, standing to tower over him.

The Sorcerer sniffed and screwed up his face in disgust, spitting to the side. I grabbed his chin and forced it toward me, boring into him with my burning gaze.

"We meet again. Tell me, what have you found, mighty Sorcerer?" My lips quirked up at the last words. They were powerful, sure, but subdued by our poisoned shackles? They were no more than mortal men.

"There's a camp nearby. I don't like the look of it." Elias jerked away, trying to wrench himself from my grasp. That only yanked on his shackles further and he yelped as the metal bit into his skin. "That's all you're getting from me, though."

"If I may, Commander," Kaine started, digging through his pockets.

I tore my gaze up away from the Sorcerer. "Go on."

"He led us to an abandoned camp not far from here. Whoever was there left not too long ago—the coals were still a bit warm, in fact. The air was thick with magic. His kind of magic." Kaine gripped his captive's shoulder tighter. Elias grimaced.

"And?" I continued. "You mean to say there's more of them? What are they after?"

"We found this," Kaine tossed a string of beads onto the table. They clattered across the smooth wood and skidded to a stop.

"Wait a second." Lucien rose. He brushed a hand over

the smooth carved beads and a rare shiver racked him. "I've seen these before. Quite recently, in fact."

The rest of the officers, myself included, turned to face him.

"I remember seeing them when I went with Alec to Steamshire, there was a woman selling them there, she had dozens of them..." His voice trailed off. Lucien's throat worked as he swallowed hard.

"You think the humans are onto us?" Kaine asked. "After your...ahem...exodus? Surely they have not taken such an affront lightly."

Lucien rubbed his chin and sunk back into his chair, still fingering the beads. "I will take them to my mate Alec and see what he has to say. He is much more familiar with the human tribes than I. But if it's true and the humans have found a way to harness magic, we're in a lump of trouble indeed."

"You have anything to say about this?" I rounded on Elias again, the new knowledge pulsing through my blood.

"I've told you everything I know. I found that stupid camp. What more do you want?"

"You'll keep tracking them." I commanded. "You'll go with Kaine here and you'll keep us informed. We can't fight a war on two fronts. Our biggest weapon right now is knowledge."

"And in return?" Elias asked, looking around at the splendor of the council hall. It was one of the few places that had not been destroyed in the battle for Darkvale, and for that I was glad.

"I've told you before. You will be safe within our walls, so long as you heed our word. That's more than you can say out in the wilds."

The Sorcerer's lip curled as if he was about to say something, then he relaxed. "Very well then. You have my word."

"A Sorcerer's word means nothing." I spat back at him. It was a risky game we were playing here, but rebel Sorcerers joining the human cause could mean devastation for our troops. "Fools talk, heroes walk."

I looked to Kaine and his cousin Ward, nodding at them. "Remove his shackles, but be on your guard. One false move..." I made a slicing motion across my neck and made sure Elias saw it.

"Don't make me regret my decision." I stared deep into his sapphire depths, ensuring the message reached all the way down to his soul.

There was a metal clank as the shackles fell away and the two guards led him out of the council hall.

A collective exhale of breath. We all looked at one another silently. "Goddess," Tork starting, rubbing the back of his neck. "We can never get rid of those bastards, can we?"

I placed my hands flat on the table and glanced at each of my men. They looked to me, waiting for direction. For answers. Even Lucien. I snapped my gaze over to my mate Nikolas, who had sat silently next to me the entire time. His eyes didn't have the far away look of someone who was bored or uninterested, though. I could nearly see the gears churning through his mind.

He was on to something.

"There's something else." Nikolas broke the silence. He fished a pen out of his pocket and started scribbling on the map before anyone had a chance to tell him no. He marked big rough X's at intervals around the fortress walls and then an arrow from one of them leading off toward the east.

"You all are outsiders—sort of, anyway. Darkvale's changed. You all know that. For the last five years, I've been here. They kept me cooped up, but I could still listen. I heard many things over those years. Heard plenty of plans, gossip, chatter. Things I wasn't supposed to hear. Not like I could do much with the info if I was locked up, right? Well, I happen to know that they planned for secret entrances and exits to the fortress. They didn't manage to finish all the tunnels, but there's one—" He tapped the map.

"It's no good," Lucien interrupted. "We blew it up during the siege. All that's there now is dust." His voice was a little harder than usual, betraying some hidden emotion I couldn't name.

"Ah," nodded Nik, "But you only got the one." He crossed out the cave-in and drew another line snaking around the perimeter and to the south. "Started out as a ventilation shaft from what I can tell."

"There are ventilation shafts all over the city," I said, furrowing my brow at Nikolas. "What makes this one any different?"

"If you'd let me finish..." Nik flicked his gaze up to mine and flashed me a teasing grin. I shut my mouth.

"This *was* a ventilation shaft, but I kept hearing this weird grinding noise in the middle of the night. Almost like they were trying to bore it out for some other reason." He struck a bold line downward, leading away from the fortress. "I say we go check it out."

Lucien and I exchanged glances. Tork cracked his knuckles. As the demolitions expert, there was nothing he loved more than blowing shit up.

"Shall we?" Tork gestured to the door, clearly ready to jump into the action.

I held up a hand as I scrutinized the map further. I looked up at Nikolas with a new sense of gratitude. As bad as I felt for leaving him behind all those years, he'd been gathering crucial information from the enemy. If there really was another tunnel open, then perhaps we weren't as safe as we thought.

And perhaps we could use it to do a little counter spying of our own.

"Wait till nightfall," I said, tracing the path of Nik's pen across the map. If it went all the way through...where would it lead? What would be waiting for us on the other side?

Only one way to find out.

"Dismissed," I waved to the officers, still staring at the map. "Tork, meet me here at sundown."

"Will do, Commander." He saluted and walked off.

As the rest of the men gathered their things and filed out of the Council Hall, I felt a pair of eyes on me. Nik's eyes.

Now that we were alone once more, a resurgence of desire crackled over my skin and left me hot, wanting. Warring emotions clashed in my mind like soldiers on a battlefield, and I didn't quite know which would win out.

Love.

Lust.

Surprise.

Admiration.

Grief.

My head buzzed with the weight of it all and left me breathless.

Nik put a hand around my waist to steady me. He nuzzled into my neck and took a long breath. I held him there for a few moments, the only feeling that of our chests rising and falling in unison.

"I've got to go," Nik whispered, resting his forehead against mine. "Lyria's playdate is over soon. Said I'd pick her up."

"Ah." The reality of it all came crashing back in on me like a ten foot wave. No matter what happened, I had something to fight for. Not only my mate, but my daughter. She deserved all the world had to offer.

"What are we gonna tell her?" I asked. "I can't very well move in right away."

"We'll take it slow. For her."

"You'll let me know what happens, right?" Nik looked up at me through his long lashes. "I wish I could go with you."

I cupped a hand around the back of Nik's neck and pulled him closer, planting a kiss on his hairline. "Take care of our girl. I'll be careful, I promise."

I won't leave you again. I projected to him when the words wouldn't come.

I know, he sent back, and we parted ways.

As I watched him leave, there was a feeling not unlike that of the most action-packed battle. It was heady, intoxicating, tingly. But not blind bloodlust, no.

Family.

12

NIKOLAS

I picked Lyria up from school just in time. She stood there with hands on her hips, clearly indignant about me being five minutes later than usual.

I took her small hand and we headed back to the house, but my normally bubbly Lyria stayed silent.

"You doing okay?" I asked her over dinner. She stared into her soup without making eye contact. I fought down the fear in my gut. If anyone hurt my girl...

"Lyria," I said again, and she finally looked up.

"You're seeing that man again." She said the words simply, matter-of-factly. Goddess, she was too perceptive for her own good. "The alpha."

I chewed my lip, trying to figure out how to explain this to her. "Yes," I said finally. "He's not so bad, you know."

"He's not my daddy. You're my daddy." She shoveled more soup into her face and broke my gaze again.

I rubbed the back of my neck. This was gonna be harder than I thought. Things were moving forward with Marlowe, but if Lyria wasn't happy...

"I'll always be your daddy, sweetheart." I reached forward to cover her hand with my own. "I'm not going anywhere, you know that. You're my little princess, and you *always* come first. Nothing's gonna change that."

She looked at me through those wide, shining eyes. "Promise?"

I gave her hand a squeeze. "Promise. Now finish your soup so we can get you cleaned up and ready for bed."

We passed the rest of the meal in silence, but the tension in the air still hung thick and heavy.

One step forward, two steps back.

———

As the sun began to wane and cast the city in its warm, sleepy glow, I heard Marlowe's voice in my mind.

How's she doing?

I gave a wry grin I knew he couldn't see and gathered my thoughts. *She's...okay.* I didn't want to worry him right before his expedition.

I would be lying if I said it had been far from my mind all evening. All the whispered snatches of conversation, all the secrets, all the things I'd gathered while in captivity came back to haunt me. What if I was wrong? What if something happened to him?

I squeezed my eyes shut.

What's wrong? You seem...disquieted.

The fact that he could tell just from the mental static on the Link unnerved me, but at the same time, I felt a little more at ease. The Marlowe that left me behind five years ago had been a harsher man. The years had done their toll on him, to be sure, but as he reached out to me I felt true concern. Even in the light of war and doubt, he found a place for me.

And that, more than anything else, brought me hope.

I'm worried about you, I admitted.

An electric jolt flashed through me, like being shocked. *As I am about you. Take care of our girl. I will be fine.*

I hope so. I thought wearily. *I sure hope so.*

Lyria emerged from the bathroom buck-naked with a pile of soap bubbles atop her head like a hat. She grinned from ear to ear and dripped water onto the floor.

Oh, crap. I was supposed to be giving her a bath, and then I'd gotten distracted by Marlowe's psychic call.

"Lyria," I breathed, wondering how she'd gotten into the

soap. I couldn't help but laugh though. She was my little girl. My baby. Even though she could be impossible sometimes, she made up for it with sheer adorableness.

"I took a bath, daddy!" She spun in a circle and bubbles went flying. I'd been so distracted worrying about Marlowe I hadn't noticed her sneak off, hadn't heard the splashes of water coming from the bathroom.

I chuckled and took her hand. "Yes you did! Let's go finish up now."

I ushered her back into the bathroom to assess the damage. Luckily, she hadn't made too big of a mess. There were splotches of water all over the floor and a spilled container of soap but nothing I couldn't clean up.

"You did a good job," I assured her, "But next time wait for daddy."

"What's wrong?" She asked sweetly.

I froze. She somehow saw through even my most valiant attempts to stay cool, calm, and collected.

"I'm fine," I said casually, brushing the soap suds off of her head.

She stayed silent while I washed her face and helped her into her clothes, but she still had a knowing look in her eye. It unnerved me and a curl of nausea roiled in my stomach. I burped loudly, tasting dinner.

Must not have sat well with me.

I had a lot on my mind, after all. I was worried about Marlowe. Worried about the tunnel and what they'd find. Worried that my intelligence wasn't correct and I'd be leading them straight into a trap. Having an over-inquisitive child? Well, that was just another addition to the already long list of stressors weighing on me.

When Lyria spoke up again she startled me from my worries. "Some of the other kids have two daddies. I guess it's not that weird." The words came out of nowhere; I had no idea she'd still been thinking about it.

I brushed hair back from her forehead and gave her a kiss. She yawned, eyes drooping.

"Marlowe likes you," I offered. "You should give him a chance."

She looked at me, confused. "Do you like him?"

Ah, the innocent questions of youth.

I turned the question over in my mind. "Yes," I said at length. "I do." A pause. "But you're always gonna be my number one girl, even if our family grows. Daddy loving someone else doesn't take any away from you. Promise."

Lyria grinned and stuck out her arms for a hug. I held her tight, feeling the warm weight of her skin and the pitter-patter of her heart. For her, I would move the world.

"Are you going to see him again?" She asked with her head on my shoulder.

"What do you say he joins us for dinner again sometime? Just the three of us."

"Okay," she agreed sleepily, and relaxed against me.

"Let's get you to bed," I whispered, and carried her to the bedroom. She curled under the covers without complaint and as she looked up at me with tired eyes, she had one more question.

"What did you mean about him being part of our family?"

I had no idea how to respond to that. She was so sweet, so innocent, laying there with a sleepy grin and the covers wrapped around her.

"We'll see," I said evenly, and kissed her good night.

13

MARLOWE

The last rays of sunlight faded over the horizon and threw the city into darkness. The air cooled, leaving with it a gentle breeze that stirred my hair and made my skin prick with gooseflesh. Shadows lengthened. The time was nigh.

Knowing that Nik was there, connected to my mind should I need him, brought me some small measure of comfort. Before when I thought Nik had died, I'd had no one. But I had a purpose much greater than that now.

"At your word, Commander," Tork said, his hot breath billowing into clouds of mist in the still air.

We'd both brought with us all manner of tools and accoutrements to scout out the mysterious tunnel. I knew deep in my heart that if the information was wrong, we'd been in for a whole heap of trouble. But if he was right...it could give us the tactical advantage we so desperately needed. Who knew where such a tunnel could lead?

Retaking Darkvale wasn't enough. We had to hold it.

And with spies and Sorcerers on the loose, not to mention vestiges of the Paradox still operating on the fringes of the world, we needed all the information we could get.

I peered at the map again, thankful for my night vision. Dragons didn't have much trouble seeing in the dark—the Goddess Glendaria had gifted us with sight when my ancestors still lived underground. Still, we were much less likely to be seen under cover of night. Less likely to be followed.

"This way," I whispered and nudged Tork to follow me. We crept along the perimeter, eyes pinned to the ground. Since Darkvale was covered with a protective dome we had ventilation shafts that brought in air from the outside. They were small, too small for anyone to fit through. But if Nik was right, they could have widened one out large enough for passage.

The usual sign of an air shaft was an old iron grate sunk into the ground, usually with grass or flowers growing around it. Lucien embarked on a beautification project some years ago before the city fell, citing that the Firefangs deserved to live in a place they were proud of. Seeing random metal grates all over the city wasn't exactly conducive to feelings of calm and comfort.

When Darkvale was under Paradox control, however, the

landscaping had totally fallen by the wayside. One would think that would make the grates easier to find if all the vegetation had wilted and perished.

Quite the opposite. Thorny, brown weeds crawled across the ground, grasping at anything they could find. It was yet another bygone facet of the Darkvale I'd once known. Teams would move on to prep the land for farming and production soon enough, I was sure, but rebuilding a city took time.

We scrambled through the morass as the weeds grew thicker. I pulled out my blade and chopped through the brush, Tork doing the same.

"You sure we're going the right way?" Tork asked. He yanked away a particularly thorny vine that left a red scratch across his cheek.

I glanced at the paper again. Any minute now, we'd be right on top of it. "Sure."

My foot stepped on something hard and I looked down, kicking aside the mess.

A discarded iron grate lay at my feet, the bars twisted and mangled by some unimaginable force. A sick feeling of fear twisted through me. What had they done?

"Well, there's the grate," I said, kicking it toward Tork. He took one look at it and grimaced the same way I did.

"But where's the tunnel?" He asked, scanning the ground with slow steps. "It's like they just tossed the grate away into the weeds—" His ankle twisted as a patch of dirt gave way. "Found something!" Tork yelled and I whirled around.

After yanking his foot free, we inspected the crack in the land. It wasn't the entrance to the tunnel, no, but someone had dug so close to the surface that the top layer had given way under Tork's weight.

"Shoddy work," Tork said, shaking his head. "Poor craftsmanship all round."

He continued muttering as we dug through the brush, looking for the entrance. I kicked an old wooden plank aside. A rough hewn hole in the earth looked back at us. It wasn't very large, no, but big enough for one person to squeeze through. Dust and dirt crumbled from the entrance as I examined it. The hole went down about five feet and then expanded south, as Nik had suggested.

"Over here," I called to Tork and he came over to inspect the tunnel. He crossed his arms and frowned. "I don't like it. Tunnel like this could give in at any moment. You saw how I knocked out the ceiling just by walking a little too heavily."

"We need to find out where it goes. If it goes anywhere, that is. Perhaps they didn't finish it."

"You're not thinking of going down there." Tork raised an eyebrow.

"Unless you want to?" I shot him a teasing grin. Pulling a

length of rope from my bag I tied it around my waist and handed an end to him. "I'm going to go check it out. You wait out here and stand watch. If you feel a yank on the rope, that's your cue to get help. Understand?"

Tork clenched his jaw but nodded. "I still don't like it."

"Didn't ask you to," I said and crouched down next to the tunnel's gaping maw. It would be a tight fit. I had a brief thought about sending a scout to explore the tunnel instead. They were smaller and quicker, meaning they could probably escape a cave-in better than I could. But I'd put enough lives on the line already.

I needed to do this myself. For Nik. For Lyria.

"I'm going in." I said, as much to myself as to him. Then I eased myself off the ledge and into the dark tunnel below.

———

It didn't take long for my eyes to adjust. Without even the moon's light, the tunnel was near pitch dark. I could still make out the rough shapes of the wall and floor, though. Whoever had come through here had done, as Tork pointed out, a "shoddy" job. They focused on speed rather than precision, as if in a last effort of desperation. I crept down the path, unreeling the length of rope as I went. I had about one hundred feet of rope on me. I figured if I ran out before coming to the end of the tunnel, I'd return to the surface and circle back with more men and supplies.

Dirt clung to the walls and floor, leaving an uneven walking surface littered with roots and stones. I sniffed the air and caught a strange metallic scent, unusual for underground. I'd smelled such a scent before, sure, at our forges. But in a hastily dug and hastily concealed tunnel? Never.

The thought spurred me on and I kept walking, keeping a hand to the right side of the wall.

I considered letting out a brief jet of dragonfire to illuminate the passage further, but I didn't want to roast myself in such an enclosed space. I unreeled more rope, felt out my next steps, and moved on.

The smell grew stronger the further I worked my way in to the tunnel. The ceiling and floor rose and fell. It was over seven feet deep in some parts, and only about five in others, making me crouch low as I walked. My curiosity drove me forward in spite of the danger, and I was nearly out of rope when I saw the glint of metal out of the corner of my eye.

The tunnel opened up onto a larger chamber and I straightened, able to stand at full height. My shoulders and back complained from the constant crouch and I stretched. The air was cooler here and thick with the scent of smoke and iron. I focused on the faint silver glint and realized with a gulp what I was looking at.

A workshop.

The magitech engineers used all manner of gadgetry

and gizmos combined with their magical energy to create fantastic inventions. And they did their best work in labs like these. Engineers pushed the boundaries of the possible and allowed us to protect ourselves, detect intruders, and devise new and interesting ways to solve problems. While dragons excelled in the magic part of magitech, our talents could only go so far. It was only through cross-species collaboration that the most advanced creations came to life.

But that was a different time, before the war.

I nearly tripped on something as I stepped into the chamber and bent down to look.

A hand.

A metal hand.

The thought chilled me all the way to my core and I looked away. I thought to yank on the rope and alert Tork when I saw something else even more damning.

Eyes. Two pale, shining eyes watching me from the darkness.

"Hey!" I screamed and lunged forward. The rope ran out and I staggered, yanking it out of Tork's hands. The eyes blinked and disappeared, fading into the blackness. Just like that, they were gone.

I spun around and drew my sword, looking for any sign of movement. Sparks rumbled through my chest and onto my tongue, looking for an outlet. Everything was still. Quiet.

Too quiet.

I heard footsteps behind me and a scattering of dust as Tork barreled into the tunnel after me.

"What are you doing?" I hissed. "You were supposed to sound the alarm, not come in after me!"

Tork's eyes were wild with fear and widened further at the sight of the metal skeletons littering the room. It was a dead-end, as far as I could tell, but I couldn't shake the thought of those shining eyes...

"Thought you were hurt," Tork said. "Thought you needed me."

I let out a breath. "Well, you're here now. What do you make of this?" I waved a hand at the workshop.

"Engineers," he nodded. "Good ones."

"I saw a pair of eyes, over there." I pointed to the spot where I'd seen the eyes. Tork squinted and even stepped over to the dark corner, waving an arm through the air as if trying to catch smoke. "There's nothing here. No secret doorway. We would have seen them."

I shivered again, not able to shake the chill. If anything happened to us, no one would know where to look. No one except Nik, anyway. I reached out to him with a thought, hoping I could at least contact him.

If you don't hear from me in an hour, get help. I'm on the south side of town past the overgrown weeds. There's a twisted iron grate nearby.

A pause.

...shhhkkktt...

Static.

No reply came, even as I waited out the harrowing moments in silence. I just had to hope he'd heard me. I projected an image of where we'd entered the tunnel. Perhaps he'd see that if nothing else. Then I came back to the present, squared my stance, and prepared for the worst.

"Watch out!" Tork cried as I stepped backward onto a pressure plate. It clicked into the ground. Too late. Noxious green gas poured out of a crack in the wall, filling the small cavern. It worked its way up my nose, into my mouth, through my lungs. My eyes watered and I coughed. I tried to release a jet of flame but none came. The air was still and bitter with the taste of magic.

I screwed up my face, trying to will the fire out of me. Nothing. No wings. No shift. No claws.

Goddess-damned Sorcerers!

"I can't shift!" Tork yelled between hacking, wheezing coughs. "Run!"

I stumbled toward the exit as my throat closed up on me.

Tork was a few paces ahead of me but by the sound of it, he wasn't faring too well either.

Just keep running, I told myself as I pushed through the pain. Not far now. Get to Nik. Get to Lyria.

A cold, numb feeling sunk into my skin and through my veins like being doused in ice water.

Each step felt like trying to wade through waist-high water. My steps slowed. The world grew dark around me as my knees gave way, and the last thing I remember thinking was *Nik. Please. Don't hurt Nik.*

14

NIKOLAS

Something was wrong. Very, very wrong.

I felt it all the way down to my soul.

Like a badly tuned radio station, I heard Marlowe in my mind. I saw an open field covered with tangled brush. I saw a gaping hole in the ground. Then nothing.

I tried to tell myself that I was overreacting. Surely he was fine.

But the nagging feeling in my gut wouldn't let go. I had to do something.

I looked over at Lyria's sleeping form and frowned. I hated to wake her, but I couldn't sit here and do nothing.

Who would I even tell? My first thought was to go to Clan Alpha Lucien himself, but he had his hands full. Him and Alec had left only today on a diplomatic mission to seek out other shifter tribes and gather allies.

Adrian was a kind omega with a beautiful young boy named Finley. We'd spoken a few times and he was exceptionally good with children. But I needed somewhere safe for Lyria while I looked for Marlowe.

There was Myrony, who had probably just finished scrubbing the plates for the night and was turning in around this time. She was a real sweetheart, but she worked so hard already.

Then there was the schoolmaster, Thomas. He was an alpha in status but treated everyone as equals, making him a perfect choice for a teacher. Since the influx of human children from Steamshire, he'd taken them under his wing. During the day him and a few other volunteers would watch over and teach the human kids alongside the shifter children. Despite the cries of panic from more traditionalist factions such as the Iron Paradox or the Elders of Steamshire, the combination had been successful for both human and shifter. Children were born without prejudice, after all.

I sighed, rummaging through my mental list of contacts. Who could I tell? Who could help? And more importantly, who would let me go after him?

During the Paradox days, omegas taking any position of initiative or power was highly frowned upon. Even though they were gone, I'd been around them for so long I'd started to internalize some of their harmful ideas. But I had to be better than that. For Marlowe, for my clan, and for my daughter.

THE DRAGON'S SECOND-CHANCE OMEGA

I gently shook Lyria awake and held her at my hip, listening to her groggy questions as I grabbed a few things from the closet.

"Where are we going, daddy?" She mumbled against my neck, and my heart nearly broke right there.

"I'm sorry, sweetheart, but we've gotta go on a little trip, okay?"

"Daddy?" She asked again, yawning.

I gulped and steeled my resolve. Leaving her would be the hardest thing. But it wasn't forever, and I trusted my clansmen.

"We're going to go see Mr. Cadbury," I soothed her as I ran a hand through her hair. "I heard he has a lot of toys at his house."

Another sleepy yawn. "It's the middle of the night."

"I know, darling. Just trust daddy, okay?"

"Okay," she whispered, but as she burrowed into my shoulder, I knew she was anything but.

———

"I'm sorry, Thomas. You know I wouldn't be here if it wasn't an emergency." I looked up into Thomas's tired and confused eyes as we stood at the threshold. He was still wearing pajamas and fluffy bunny slippers.

I lowered my voice and leaned in closer. "Marlowe's missing. I think I know what happened to him."

Tom's face blanched. "Come on in." He opened the door wider and we stepped inside.

True to my word, Tom's place was full of storybooks, blocks, and other toys. Though he didn't have kids of his own, he often ran a daycare for kids in the school program out of his house. I set Lyria down next to the building blocks and Thomas followed me into the kitchen.

"What is this about, Nikolas?" He asked in barely more than a whisper. "Have you any idea what time it is?"

"I do, and that's why I need your help."

Thomas crossed his arms. "By watching your little one while you go off to play the hero?"

I clenched my jaw. "Look, I know what I'm doing. I know where he is, I know where to find him. It has to be me." When he continued to look at me like that I added, "I'll be careful. I promise."

"Lyria needs her father," he warned. "Don't go doing anything stupid. Take someone with you, at least."

"Fine, I just...I need to go. My mate's in danger and I can't sit here and do nothing."

His eyes lit up as if remembering some far-off memory. "I'll watch her. You go get your mate." He clapped me on the back. "But don't say I never did you any favors."

"You're a lifesaver, man. I'll make it up to you, promise."

Tom shooed me away and I gave Lyria a last hug and kiss before we separated and I headed for the door.

"I'll be back soon," I promised Tom. "No more than a few hours, tops. If I'm not back by sunup, well..."

"I'll get in touch with Lucien."

"Thanks."

I turned my gaze inward, looking through the bits and pieces I'd picked up over our Link. It was still early days, still weak from the years of neglect, but I could see enough. The words were mostly garbled, but I could make a few of them out. South...weeds...gate...

He'd gone for the tunnel.

I took off at a run, trying to reach out to him in my mind. No response. That made me run faster, and I nearly ran right into one of the Firefangs in my path. The man dropped a toolbox with a clank and wobbled on his feet, looking at me wide-eyed.

"Whoa, where are you going so fast?" It was Ansel making his nightly rounds to maintain the magitech wards over the city. He wore glasses and had perpetually mussed hair. If you got him started talking about engineering, he'd talk your ear off, but was normally pretty silent.

"Can't talk now, Ansel. Gotta run." I took a few steps

then skidded to a halt with an idea. "Actually, follow me. Need your help."

"Wha?" He started but I grabbed his sleeve and yanked him along.

"Tell you on the way!" I yelled as we set off to the south.

———

"Wait, so you mean to say there's been a secret tunnel here all this time and no one thought to tell me?" Ansel breathed heavily as he tried to keep up. I couldn't tell if the deflated tone of his voice was from fatigue or if he was actually hurt.

"Recent discovery," I clipped. The weeds were growing thicker now, and we fought through the brambles in the footsteps of the men who had come before us. "Marlowe didn't come out here alone," I mused as I eyed the sets of footprints. "Tork, that's who it was."

Ansel gave a little squeak as he quickened his pace to keep up. I could have sworn I saw the hint of a blush creep up his cheeks, but it was too dark to really tell.

"You work with him, don't you?" I remembered now that Tork worked in the engineering department too.

"Something like that," he muttered and looked away. He pointed to the discarded metal grate. "There!"

I sucked in a breath as we approached the entrance. It

wasn't far from the grate, and whatever had happened to that poor piece of iron, it wasn't pretty.

The entrance was visible enough—there were skid marks where the men had slid into the tunnel but not a clear way back out. I called down into the depths at the top of my voice.

"Marlowe! Tork! You in there?"

My voice echoed off the walls. Nothing.

"You smell something?" I said suddenly, wrinkling my nose.

It took only a second for Ansel to go into full-on panic mode. "Shit, it's emerald gas!" He covered his face with his hand and fished out a mask, throwing it to me. "Quick!"

I'd never seen the normally calm Ansel look so afraid. I wasted no time strapping it to my face and breathed a clean breath in through the filter. "What's going on?" I asked in a muffled voice as Ansel fitted his own mask.

"The tunnel's poisoned! We gotta get them out of there!"

Before he could finish his sentence I leapt into the tunnel and skidded to a stop on the rough dirt-packed floor. Ansel wasn't far behind me, his eyes still wide with alarm.

"Come on," I urged him, and we ran.

I continued to call out their names, the only sounds that

of my voice reflected back to me off the uneven walls. I thought back to the grinding, scraping sounds I'd heard in the middle of the night so many times. This must have been what they were working on. But why? And why so hastily?

"Marlowe!" I yelled again through my mask.

"Tork!" Ansel called.

It wasn't long until we found them.

I rushed forward, my heart in my throat. They lay collapsed on the floor, unmoving. I bent down to check for a pulse. Good, they were still alive.

"Got any more of those masks?" I asked Ansel as I struggled to roll Marlowe over.

"I'm fresh out," Ansel wrung his hands and glanced down the tunnel. "It's coming from in there. We've got to plug the source before it reaches the surface!"

I froze with fear. Oh, *shit*. If the gas was that powerful, and that deadly, could it knock out an entire city?

"I'll get them out. Can you plug the leak?"

Ansel nodded, digging through his tool bag. "I'm on it."

We locked glances for a brief moment. No matter what people said about omegas, they could be damn resourceful in times of need.

Especially when it came to their mates.

I crouched down and hooked my arms under Marlowe's armpits, groaning as I lifted him into a sitting position. He must weigh twice what I did!

"You start getting sick, you get out. Get help. You hear?" Ansel warned with a last glance at Tork.

"Same," I nodded. "Now go!"

He took off at a run, and I was left alone with two unconscious alphas.

15

NIKOLAS

"Wake up," I projected at Marlowe through our Link. "Wake up, wake up, wake up—damn you're heavy!"

Are you trying *to dislocate my shoulder?*

I let out a breath as I heard his response in my mind. Marlowe's eyes fluttered open, widening as he saw me there. His face no longer had the ruddy gleam it usually did. Even his eyes, once shining with the light of the fire within him, were no more than dull embers.

This was bad.

"What are you..." he started but cut short in a fit of coughs.

"Saving your ass," I responded and offered him my hand. "Come on!"

I braced myself against the wall and pulled, Marlowe stumbling upright at last. Sweat already started to bead up on my forehead, and we weren't out of the woods yet. Marlowe leaned against the wall, heaving and shaking as he ejected the contents of his stomach. The smell mixed with the cloying emerald gas nearly made me gag, even through the protective mask.

Marlowe wiped his mouth with the side of his hand and looked to his fallen comrade.

"Help me," I commanded, pulling at Tork's jacket to turn him over.

Marlowe could barely stand, though, let alone lift another person. I had to do this myself.

There was a crack and the sound of a muffled explosion from down the tunnel and I bit my lip, hoping it was Ansel stopping the gas leak and not getting blown up himself.

No time to think about that, though.

"Stay close to the wall and run." I squeezed Marlowe's hand as our eyes connected. A fraction of the fire returned and he set his jaw, nodding.

"Go, I'm right behind you!" I yelled and pushed him away. Marlowe staggered down the tunnel away from me and away from the gas.

Now there was just the matter of Tork.

I'll never be able to lift him, my mind wailed as I dug in my heels and struggled to get him upright. I called his name over and over, but he wouldn't wake. He was still breathing, slowly, raggedly, but breathing. For now.

I didn't know how much longer he had.

As I narrowed my eyes and the world fell away, I felt a rush of strength surge through my muscles. I had to do this. No other choice.

You saved me, the faint voice echoed through my mind. *Save him too. Take my strength, get him out of there.*

A dozen firecrackers went off inside my body all at once. I let out a roar and heaved, Tork's body coming off the ground. My eyes widened as I froze for only a moment, stunned at myself.

Go! I heard Marlowe's voice again, and I looped one of Tork's arms around my shoulder, dragging him toward the exit.

Footsteps pattered behind me and Ansel emerged. His face was drawn, dirty, and sweaty, but he was alive. Without a word he took Tork's other arm and lightened my load. With Tork's weight distributed between us, we moved faster this time, our own breaths coming in shallow gasps from the exertion.

Tork still wasn't awake, and despite my newfound strength the dead weight was anything but easy to carry. I set my sights on the goal and kept moving. It was all we could do.

Neither of us said anything. Couldn't. Too focused in the moment, the only thing that mattered was the tiny point of light at the end of the tunnel.

Freedom.

Safety.

And not dying in this poisonous cave.

A hand shot out as we neared the ragged hole that marked the exit. Then a rope. Voices echoed down into the cave.

We pushed on the last few yards even as the world began to darken around me. My head swum, my vision blurred, and the strangest fluttering sensation seized my stomach.

I grabbed on to the rope and held on for dear life. The volunteers had arrived.

I felt cool grass under my feet and saw the prone form of Tork and Ansel lying, exhausted, on the ground. The volunteers shoveled dirt into the hole and covered it with the grate, then at last we could breathe once more.

I looked to Marlowe, who leaned against a tree and was being tended by two healers. They lifted Tork onto a makeshift gurney to do the same.

Safe.

The price of the harrowing rescue caught up with me at last. My muscles ached. My stomach roiled. I couldn't see. My dragon took hold and smothered out the light as I collapsed, soundless, onto the ground.

16

MARLOWE

The fact that I could barely breathe was secondary.

My mate had saved my life, and now he'd collapsed in front of me.

I pulled myself away from the healers, their squawking cries no more than background noise.

"Nik," I breathed, brushing a lock of hair from his face. "I need a healer!"

"Damn right you do, now stay still!" Meryl grabbed my arm and reattached the air-filtering mask. "We've got to remove the toxins in your lungs, hun."

My dragon roared from deep within and I nearly swiped the mask away again. "You've got to help him!" I pointed at Nik, still laying unconscious.

"We will, but you've got to let us do our job." Kyva, the

other healer nearby, sidestepped me to crouch down next to Nik. She hovered a hand over his face, taking a few long, deep breaths. A gentle golden light emanated from her palm and washed over him. Kyva's eyes flicked back and forth as if she was reading something, but I could see no inscription. Then her eyes widened in surprise.

She turned to look at me with a raised eyebrow and then gestured to Meryl. "Get both of them inside, now."

She slapped me on the back as she moved on to evaluate Ansel, but I couldn't get that expression of surprise off her face. What was she hiding?

"Come along now," Meryl prodded me toward a nearby shelter. "Let's get you somewhere more private."

My blood ran cold at her words. Private? What could have been so bad? I looked over to Nik again, still unmoving. A lump forced itself into my throat and I tasted bile. What if...I shuddered from head to foot. What if he wasn't going to make it?

My dragon didn't like that idea one bit and it reared inside of me, smoke pouring from my nostrils as I ran to Nik's side again. A dull, throbbing pain shot up my leg with each step and I was sure to feel even more sore once the adrenaline wore off, but Nik needed me.

I wouldn't leave him to suffer alone again.

I'm here, Nik, I projected to him over our Link. No

response came. I squeezed his hand, still hanging limp by his side. I'll take care of you.

Another healer came by carting a gurney for Nik and looked me up and down. "You the omega's mate?" He asked.

"Yes," I said and tightened my grip on Nik's hand.

"I'm Nolan. Come with me."

Him and an assistant lifted Nikolas carefully onto the gurney and pushed him into a small shelter where two more healers waited.

"What's going on?" The healers converged on him, speaking in hushed tones and working quickly with practiced motions of the hand.

Nolan approached, appraising me over the wire rims of his glasses. He spoke slowly, weighing the importance of each word.

"His dragon, as a means of protection, has gone into hibernation. Not unlike the Dragonheart Curse, shifters in times of crisis can go into a coma-like state as their beast fights to restore balance. It's not harmful...usually... but we'll need to keep an eye on him, just in case."

"Nik," my voice came out as a croak. I stepped toward him and lay a hand on his forehead. His eyes were closed, staring at nothing. Breaths came in and out slowly, his chest rising and falling. This was all my fault.

If only I'd escaped faster...

If only I'd brought more backup.

If only I hadn't failed him once again.

"But he'll be all right?" I asked, almost fearing the answer. "You can fix him?"

Nolan rubbed his chin and conferred with the two healers working over Nik's prone body.

He paused, taking a breath, then continued. "Chances are good, and our healers are top-notch, you know that. But there is a...complication." Nolan rubbed the back of his neck, eyes darting around the room.

"Well what is it?" I burst out, not able to take the silence.

"He's pregnant."

All the world screeched to a halt as I heard those two simple words. I blinked at Nolan a few times, registering his words.

Pregnant...oh, *Goddess*.

"Makes sense why his dragon retracted. It's gotta protect the little one, after all."

"Wh-what do I do?" I was used to being in charge. Being the tough guy, the warrior. Nothing fazed me. Until this omega came along. Now he'd brought down all my walls, and I would do anything just to see him wake again.

"He has a daughter, yes? She'll need to be informed."

My throat stuck together like that time I ate too much honey. Oh no. *Lyria*. How could I break this kind of news to the girl? Even if I was her daddy too, we'd hardly gotten to know each other.

"Wh-what do I do?" I was used to being in charge. Being the tough guy, the warrior. Nothing fazed me. Until this omega came along. Now he'd brought down all my walls, and I would do anything just to see him wake again.

I ran a hand through my hair and let out a sigh. Guess we were going to be spending a lot more quality time together.

"You don't happen to know where she is, do you?" Darkvale wasn't *that* big, but I still didn't have any idea where to start.

"I don't, but ask around. I'm sure someone's seen her."

I took a last longing glance at Nik and leaned down to plant a kiss on his forehead. *I'm so sorry*, I mindspoke to him, even though I knew I'd get nothing in return. *I'll come back for you soon.*

"Let the healers work. Go find the girl," Nolan suggested, and I stepped out of the shelter into the rising sun.

———

The first rays of dawn spread out across the city, reflected in prisms of light through the protective dome that kept Darkvale safe. The giant orb of fire was only a sliver on the horizon. Already the land was awash in gold and red as the light banished the darkness for yet another day.

At any other time, it would have been beautiful.

As it stood, it reminded me of only one thing: time was running out.

Thoughts sped through my mind quicker than I could run. The filtration mask had done quick work, but I still felt a little hoarse.

The bitter tang of metal stuck to my tongue, a constant companion as I rushed across town. Where could she be?

The early risers of the Firefangs were only just now starting their day, and they looked at me with tired eyes and confused expressions when I asked (albeit a bit frantically) if they'd seen Lyria.

No one had.

After the fifth rejection, I stopped a moment to reconsider my strategy. If she truly was my daughter, then we'd have a Link connection too, right? It would be weak, for sure, but she was my flesh and blood. If I could just seek that out...

There.

A faint, vibrating energy called to me out of the east. It was almost imperceptible, and it probably would have been had I not been specifically looking for it. I couldn't hear much or see anything at all, but I had a feeling. And that was enough of a start.

I turned and followed the source, letting her light lead me like a compass. Follow your instincts, my old master used to say. They will show you the path.

When I ended up in front of Thomas's quarters, I kicked myself for not thinking of it sooner. Some lovingly called him the 'clan daddy' for how much he cared for the little ones. Him and the other volunteers at the makeshift school spent all their time and energy preparing both shifters and humans alike for a better life.

It only made sense that Thomas would be the one to take her in.

I raised my hand to knock but the door opened before I had a chance.

"Thomas," I breathed. He stood there with an arched eyebrow and a poorly concealed mask of worry. "How did you—"

"You sneak about as well as a goat with tin shoes. Get in here."

He shooed me inside and shut the door.

I saw Lyria out of the corner of my eye, hands grabbing at a bowl of cereal on the table.

Thomas pulled me into the kitchen, looking me up and down. "What's this about, Marlowe? Where's Nikolas?"

I ran a hand through my hair. There was no easy way to say this, was there? "He saved my life. There was an emerald gas leak and I passed out. Tork too. But he and Ansel came and dragged us out. Saved us."

"Goddess," Thomas breathed, leaning back against the wall. "Emerald gas is nasty stuff. Where were you?"

"We found a secret tunnel on the edge of town. It's all cleared out by now, but someone was using it as a workshop right under our noses. The gas was there as a trap, and I accidentally triggered it."

"And Nik?" Thomas asked, his face growing increasingly fearful. "Did he—?"

I licked my lips, trying to find the right words. "He dragged us out of the tunnel and then collapsed. The healers say his dragon..." I stopped, my throat closing up. "...has gone into hibernation. They don't know when he's gonna wake up." I shoved my hands in my pockets and stared at the ground.

Even saying the words lanced a pain through my heart so sharp I winced. When I ran five years ago, I closed myself off to avoid the pain and fear. Now I was feeling it full force, and I felt ready to drown with the intensity of it.

Thomas let out a slow, shaky breath. "Glendaria save us."

"That's not all," I grimaced, wringing my hands. "He's pregnant, Tom."

Thomas's eyebrows reached for his hairline. He shook his

head and scrubbed a hand over his face. He took off his glasses, rubbing them on his shirt, then blinked at me through them again.

"How far along?"

"Don't know. They told me to come get Lyria, take her to him. Came as soon as I could."

The schoolmaster walked to the closet and pulled out a spherical decanter and two glasses, pouring us a few fingers each of a dark, smoky spirit.

"Here, drink." He pushed the glass at me. "You look like you need it."

"Thanks," I said wearily as I downed the stuff in one go. It burned through me from head to toe, but unlike my dragon fire it dulled the pain, terror, and hurt. Everything became just a little easier to bear.

"There is a silver lining in all of this, you know." Thomas sipped at his drink slowly, savoring the smoky aroma where I just wanted it to start working as quick as possible.

I scoffed and my dragon riled inside me. How could he say such a thing? "What's that?"

Thomas tilted his head toward the living room. "Now's your chance to be the alpha father she never had."

A crash sounded from the other room and he stood at once to find Lyria now wearing her food. She'd knocked over the bowl and soggy lumps of cereal peppered not only her face but also the table and floor.

Lyria froze, eyes wide as her lip trembled with fear. She looked at the mess and her breathing quickened. When she caught my eye, she began to wail.

I sat the glass down with a clunk on the table. Alphas didn't back down. That had always been my motto, but the fight I faced now was scarier than anything I'd seen on the battlefield. I needed to be there not only for my mate, but for my daughter and my unborn child.

I leapt into action and joined Thomas in the living room where he started cleaning and I tried to soothe Lyria. I brushed a hand through her hair and squatted so that I was eye level with her. She had the beautiful amber orbs of her father, no less brilliant in their light. She'd grow up to be a fine dragon.

"Hey, it's all right, iskra. No harm done." The word for 'spark' came to my mind in our language, and I used it to get her attention. It fit her. All energy and life and potential. My little spark.

"Where's daddy?" Lyria sniffed, pulling away from Tom's attempts to wipe her face.

I swallowed the lump in my throat and held her gaze, reaching for that pinpoint of energy I'd sensed earlier. *It's going to be okay*, I projected.

I knew it, she sent back, astonished. *You* are *my daddy!*

I heard her small voice through the Link. I froze, not expecting to hear anything in return. She knew I was her dad. She felt it, same as I did. The feeling bolstered me for what I had to say next.

"That's right, iskra." I said the words aloud. "I'm your alpha daddy. You can call me Papa, though. Your Daddy is sleeping right now. He's hurt and needs to heal. But I'm here, and you'll never be alone. We need to go see him so he can feel our love. It will be sad to see him hurt and sleeping, but he needs us. Can you be a brave dragon for Papa?"

She stared at me, her food all but forgotten. That tiny pink lip quivered as she tried to be strong. It broke my heart in all the worst ways—there was nothing I wouldn't do to bring a smile to my little girl's face again.

"Come here, iskra." I held out my arms. "I think we both need a hug."

Lyria held my gaze for a long moment, the stubbornness in her eyes conflicting with her need for reassurance. Finally she flung herself at me, throwing those small arms around my neck and burying her face in my shirt. She was so small in my arms, so delicate. A rush of warmth and emotion flooded through me all the way down to my soul as I held her. There it was. A true bond forged between us for the first time.

"There's one more thing," I said, brushing my hand

through her hair. "You're gonna be a big sister soon. Do you know what that means?"

"We're getting a dog?"

I laughed. "No, not a dog. Daddy's pregnant. He's going to have a baby, and you'll have a new brother or sister."

"Whoa..." Lyria gasped and clung to me tighter. "When?"

"A few months from now."

I had no idea how I was gonna handle this whole fatherhood thing, especially with another baby on the way. I didn't even have Nik to help me out. But I knew as I held my daughter in my arms that I would do whatever it took to make this child feel safe and loved.

"Let's get your things," I stroked a hand down her back as her breathing slowed. "Then we can go see Daddy. Say goodbye to Mr. Cadbury, okay?"

When she broke away, an odd void filled her place. I knew how Nik made me feel, sure, but a child's love was different. So pure. I watched her go and snapped myself out of it long enough to pick up her things.

"Come back and see me sometime," Thomas smiled at her. "And don't forget to take these cookies with you!" He handed her a box of sweets. "I can't eat them all by myself, now can I?"

Lyria grinned and took the box, holding it close to her

chest. "Thank you Mr. Cadbury." She shot me a mischievous glance.

"Any time, Lyria. Any time."

He waved and I gave Tom a weary look.

I wasn't sure if she picked up something from my conversation with Tom or if she was just shocked into silence but Lyria didn't say another word as we left the schoolmaster's house.

Now the hard part began.

17

NIKOLAS

I had a feeling I wasn't in Darkvale anymore.

I floated on endless clouds of cotton, adrift in a sea with no beginning and no end. Thoughts and sensations came and went, passing me by like ships in the night.

It was like the most surreal dream I'd ever had, but I was strangely lucid. I stretched out my fingers and toes, looking down at my body. Two arms, two legs. A haze of sleepy green light fluttered past my eyelids then left as soon as it came. I tried to turn my head but I stood rooted to the spot.

Where was I?

My mouth opened, but made no sound. It was like floating, no, falling, through a vacuum. Completely airless, directionless, lifeless.

Was this the Great Beyond the shamans so often spoke of? Was I dead?

I furrowed my brow trying to bring up the most recent memory I could. Last thing I remembered was pulling Marlowe out of that poisonous pit he got himself stuck in.

I was tired, sure, but I'd been lucky enough to have a filtration mask from Ansel to block out the negative effects of the gas. Marlowe, on the other hand, wasn't looking so well.

I remembered looking around for him, reaching out to grab his hand, then the world fell away.

The ground crumbled, reality evaporated. And here I was, suspended in time and space with no notion how I got here, or how I might leave.

Flames flickered around me, lapping at my skin, my clothes, my hair. The heat was warm, though not searing. I should have burnt up a thousand times by now. I turned inward, asking my dragon for answers.

No response.

Instead I felt a tiny, almost imperceptible kick, right around my abdomen. It was the strangest feeling, like something was *moving* inside of me. And not just my MIA dragon, either.

I reached out for my dragon again and felt only air. The void crushed in around me, sucking out all the light. The flames died down, and I was alone.

18

The closer we got to the healers, the more strongly I could feel Lyria's pain. It mirrored my own. Neither of us knew what was going to happen, but we were going to face it together.

"Want a ride?" I asked, holding out my arms.

She tilted her head in question.

"On my shoulders." I pointed. "You'll be able to see better from there."

Lyria wrapped her arms around me and I lifted her up and over my head, straddling her legs around my neck. She wobbled and grabbed onto my face.

"Wow, you're strong!" She screeched, taking in the view from above. "I can see everything!"

I chuckled. "We're all strong in our own ways. Even you."

"Even me?" She gasped, flexing one of her small arms.

"You're going to be quite the dragon when you grow up, you know that?" I adjusted her on my shoulders till we were both comfortable.

"That's what Daddy says, too."

"That's cause it's true, iskra." The feeling of her tiny hands on me set off a spiral of happiness. I knew well the pride that came from winning a battle, but this was a different sort of victory. A personal one. The pride and connection I felt with this little one stirred deep into my chest and my dragon adored her.

Ours, it roared in delight.

"How's that?" I asked, craning my neck upward. "Ready to go see Daddy?"

"Ready," she said, and pointed west like a captain commanding her troops. I grinned and took off toward the healers, my heart still beating in double time.

Please let them be safe.

———

"Is Daddy going to be okay?" She asked out of nowhere as we drew closer. I nearly stumbled on a rock. Lyria had caught me off guard with her question. My heart thrummed in my chest and roared in my ears, the fears I'd worked so hard to control roaring back. Was he?

I chewed my lip for a few seconds in thought. "I don't know, iskra. But that's why he needs us."

"Can we help?" Lyria asked.

"We can," I agreed. "Daddy might be sleeping, but we need to be there for him. Can you do that?"

"Yes, Papa."

"Good."

We approached the makeshift hospital at long last and I helped her off my shoulders. She looked up at me with windswept hair and a wavering smile. Her eyebrows crept upward.

"Daddy's in there?" She pointed to the burgundy canvas, worn and dusty from the winds. The color took me back to my wartime days. That red always signified a field medic—the cloth was dyed to mask the deep crimson of blood.

The entry way flapped open from an errant breeze and I could see nurses and healers moving about inside. I didn't, however, catch a glance of my mate in those few seconds.

"Yes, he's in there," I said, taking her hand. "Ready?"

She stalled, clinging to my sleeve. I heard the fear in our Link before she voiced it. "I'm scared. What are they doing to him? When is he coming home?"

"They're making sure he gets better, and they're making

sure the baby is okay. They're very smart, so we should trust them. They've patched me up more than a few times, too. And I'm all right."

We pushed through the doorway and the nurse directed us to Nik's cot. She pulled aside some curtains to give us a little privacy and then left us with him.

Lyria toddled over to his bedside. "Daddy?" She said softly.

Lyria looked back at me and then fixed her gaze on Nik again. Her mouth hung open, lip trembling as she stared at his unmoving form.

"I love you, Daddy." She lay her head on his rising and falling chest.

Emotion tugged at my chest and I squinted my eyes, suddenly burning with unbidden tears. I sniffed and shook my head.

I rested a hand over Nik's own, his skin still flushed and warm in his comatose state. I tried to project to him again, but it was like shouting into a void. He was in his own little world now, cut off from our own. The healers kept him stable, but his mind and soul were elsewhere.

The thought that maybe, wherever he was right now he could hear me gave me a small measure of comfort. As far as I knew, only one thing could wake a sleeping dragon.

Time. How much was anyone's guess.

I eyed my pregnant mate's belly, only starting to swell under the blankets. Dragon pregnancies were notoriously short—only three months. We liked to say that dragon babes were just so eager to meet the world, they couldn't wait the full nine that human babes did. What if Nikolas wasn't awake by the time the baby came?

I love you, I projected over and over again. *My best friend. My forever mate. I love you. I love you. I'm sorry. I'm ready to be the mate, and the father, this family needs.*

A tear crept free of my eyelid and dripped down onto Nik's face, leaving a wet trail.

On instinct I leaned down and kissed him, the lips unmoving against my own. But I could still breathe his scent, feel the connection of our dragons there. Buried deep within him, sleeping, but alive.

"I love you," I whispered aloud, breaking the kiss.

"He's due for his medicine," A nurse said, holding a vial of blue liquid. "And then he needs to rest."

I tore myself away from him reluctantly, every fiber of my being still crying out to be next to him. But the healers had to do their job, and I had to take care of Lyria.

"Ready to go home?" I asked Lyria, and she gave his hand a last squeeze.

"Do you think he heard us?" Lyria wondered.

"I'm sure he did." I assured her. Mates were two halves of a soul, bound together inseparably by the mating of their dragons. Surely a little barrier like consciousness wouldn't stop us, right?

19

MARLOWE

We were walking down the road back toward Nik's place when I heard it.

A small bell jingled and the shouts of a traveler rung out as an overloaded wagon trundled down the road. I craned my neck to get a better vantage point, but I couldn't see anything, just a mass of dust kicked up on the road. By someone, or something.

"What's that sound?" Lyria asked.

Children of humans and shifters alike flew past us, their parents chasing in their wake.

"The Rose Festival's starting!" A girl with messy red curls screeched as she swooped past me.

Goddess, it was here already?

I suppressed a chuckle. The first time Nik ever asked me out, it was to the Rose Festival. A Darkvale tradition, it

177

was the one time a year when merchants came from all over the realm, flowers and delicacies of every kind could be found, and the Firefangs celebrated food and family.

We've come full circle, I thought to myself with a grin.

Lyria still gazed up at me with excited eyes. Exhaustion reached all the way to my bones and the early wave of merchants always drew the most customers. I had no desire to push past the throngs of people and buy things I didn't need, but I couldn't say no to the look on her face.

A festival was a big event for a child. It often made their day, week, hell, their whole year. I remember how much I looked forward to them and the giddy gleam of excitement when the first caravans rolled into town.

Besides, it would give me a distraction from worrying about Nik, and it would lift Lyria's spirits at the same time. Win-win.

"Let's go find out," I grinned to Lyria and lifted her onto my shoulders as we joined the exodus of people heading for the gate.

Score one Good Dad point for Marlowe.

The first merchant had indeed made his way down the road and approached Darkvale, his caravan sagging with all manner of plants, flowers, and herbs of just about every shape and color I could think of. Even some I couldn't.

Lyria watched with the rest of the crowd, her eyes large

as saucers. The merchant was old, with a few tufts of white hair and a speckled face. He had friendly green eyes and a long tufted beard he wore a few shining baubles in. All the hair from his head had migrated downward, it seemed. He gave us a gap-toothed smile and waved a meaty hand as he pulled his horses to a stop.

A creaking hand-painted sign swung back and forth from the side of his wagon. Abernathy's Apothecary, it read.

And I supposed this must be Abernathy.

"There's so many!" Lyria gasped as she took in the bundles of flowers spilling over the sides of the caravan. Indeed, this was quite the harvest. My last Rose Festival was my first date with Nik, to be fair, but I hadn't remembered how resplendent it all was.

For those of us who had little else, a festival of food, family, and exotic delights could brighten the darkest mood.

"Can we get something, Papa?" Lyria asked excitedly.

I eyed the rows of colorful flowers, thinking again of Nik. Before becoming mates, we'd been childhood friends. Those were simpler days, spent lounging in the sun or playing hide and seek with the other kids. Nik had always had an eye for color, and it pained my heart that he wasn't here to see this.

That doesn't mean he has to completely miss out, I

reasoned. *The room the healers kept him in was so awfully dull. Why can't we brighten it up?*

"How about we get some flowers for daddy?" I proposed.

"Good idea," Lyria agreed. "And we can make flower crowns too!"

I blinked. Flower...crowns? I'd never heard of such a thing. "What's that?" I asked.

"I saw some of the girls making them at daycare. They're so pretty...you weave flowers together and wear them. I wanted one, but they ran out." Her lip stuck out in an adorable pout.

"A crown for my princess it is, then." Lyria bounced with excitement and I couldn't help it, I got a little giddy myself. Even in the midst of crisis, her spirit was infectious.

And I could get used to that.

"Let's see what they have." I wove through the crowd to get a better look, Lyria taking in all the blooms from above.

"Why hello there." Abernathy waved, looking at us over his ancient spectacles. "It's good to see this fortress alive again."

"You can say that again," I agreed, and my dragon roared with triumph. "The Firefang clan and their human allies have returned home to Darkvale, and we intend to stay."

Abernathy's bushy mustache bristled as he shook his head in wonder. "I must say, humans and shifters living together...I've traveled far across this world and never seen such a thing. How do you manage?"

"The world is changing," I said proudly. "We change along with it. Our Clan Alpha mated a human, for instance."

"My word."

"Through working together, we build something greater than ourselves." I recited the Firefang creed to him. "We share this land with all our brothers and sisters, not only those of our flesh and blood."

The merchant gave us a surprised but warm smile. "It warms my heart to see. And what's good for you is good for me, as well. Good for my wallet, too." He gave us a wink. "See anything you like? Perhaps a trinket for the darling girl?"

He produced a smooth ivory shell seemingly from nowhere, gleaming in the light and carved into a perfect heart shape. "For the little princess." He offered it up to Lyria and she clutched at it with wide, awestruck eyes.

"Thank you," I bowed my head to Abernathy before continuing. We were here on a mission, after all. "I've got something of a special request."

"Do tell," Abernathy's eyes twinkled with curiosity.

"My mate is very sick, hibernating in fact, and I thought we might bring him some flowers."

"Say no more!" The merchant cried as he rushed through a curtain into his stores. "I've just the thing!"

I let Lyria down from my shoulders as we exchanged confused glances. She hugged the ivory carving to her chest, still admiring the smooth milky surface that shone in the light.

What Abernathy returned with was even more stunning.

A brightly colored bouquet emerged from the wagon, resplendent in reds and golds, the petals each perfectly shaped as if by a master artist. It looked too precious to be real.

"This is the rulo flower," he said in a reverent tone. "Came from all the way across the sea, very exotic, very rare even in those parts. Early explorers used to mistake it for gold, if you can believe it." He stroked the metallic petals. "Imagine their surprise when they found it was simply a flower!"

"It's pretty," Lyria breathed, just as enraptured as I was.

"Pretty, yes, but that's not all. The real magic lies within." He peeled back one of the delicate petals to reveal a cache of pollen at the center, glittering like tiny diamonds.

"The pollen that the rulo flower produces is said to bring vitality, abundance, and good fortune." He took a whiff of the bouquet and gave us a satisfied smile. "In fact, they say this was the Goddess's favorite flower when she walked these realms so long ago. That she's said to bless anyone in their presence. And if that's not enough," he wiggled his eyebrows, "It's also known as The Lover's Bloom. I'll let you figure that one out yourself." He gave me a wink.

Heat rose to my cheeks and I hoped Lyria didn't notice. I knew merchants were always out to make a sale, but what could I say? They were perfect.

"How much?" I asked, internally cringing at what I knew would be an exorbitant price.

Abernathy stepped back, holding the bouquet to his chest as if protecting it. His gaze bored into mine, those green eyes flashing. He studied me from head to toe, as if looking for something beyond just my body. As if he were looking *inside*. I shivered, suddenly uneasy.

Then the merchant spoke again.

"This is one of my most exotic finds. You must understand I cannot let it go easily." He looked lovingly down at the bouquet then back to me, his gaze no less intense. "But I have seen your heart is true."

"What are you talking about?"

He continued in that same eerie tone, yet I couldn't deny it: everything he said was true. "You've been through many trials, yes. But many are still to come, Peter

Marlowe." He considered me for another long pause as the beating of my startled heart counted the seconds. "I've traveled a long way. Longer than you know. But I believe the Goddess has led me here for a reason, and I heed her cosmic signs. We were meant to meet this day. Of that I am sure. Take these flowers as my gift to you, and send my best wishes to your mate."

I blinked, muscles relaxing only a little. "I couldn't," I said warily. "Let me pay you—"

"I wouldn't hear of it," Abernathy insisted, pressing the bundle of flowers into my reluctant hands. "Though..." He continued, rubbing his beard. "If you wish to buy something else I wouldn't say no..." He regarded us both with a wink and a friendly grin, and my dragon uncoiled little by little.

He was just a kooky old man.

I snapped my gaping jaw shut and turned to Lyria. "While we're here, how about we get some seeds for the garden? You'll have to help me pick out the best ones, though."

"Thank you," I mouthed to Abernathy and Lyria led me away.

———

A bit of haggling and an exchange of gold coins later, we

had seeds for tomatoes, corn, potatoes, rosemary, and sage.

Oh, and a rare bouquet of impossibly pretty flowers.

"Ready to go home?" I asked Lyria, who was sucking on a maple candy she'd conned me into buying for her. I hefted my bags in one hand, teetering a bit as I balanced everything just right. Then I took Lyria's small hand in my own and we pushed our way out of the growing crowds.

If there were this many people gathered for such an early arrival, I couldn't imagine what the festival would be like in full swing.

As we walked back home hand in hand, an unfamiliar feeling shone down on me like the sun. For the first time ever, I didn't feel that urge to run away or drown myself in battle. I liked this feeling, this calm, confident assurance that I felt when I was around her. When I was around Nik. The warmness of gratitude bubbled through me and filled me up, my dragon coiling and uncoiling as he took all of it in.

No more running. This time I had something worth staying for.

Family.

.

20

MARLOWE

I f someone had told me a year ago that the rough and tough commander Peter Marlowe would be kneeling at a too-small table making flower crowns with a little girl, I would have laughed in their face.

But now? There was nowhere I'd rather be.

I'd changed a lot since then, I mused as my fat fingers struggled with the stiff vines. We all had.

"No, no, no! It's like this, see?"

Lyria grabbed the mangled flower stems from my hand and twisted one over the other, linking them together so that the blooms formed a crescent shape.

"That's what I was doing," I complained.

"You were doing it wrong."

"How's this?" I offered. It was still a bit wilty, but hey, I tried.

Lyria regarded my attempt and shrugged. "Better."

No one ever told me there was a "right" way to make a flower crown. But apparently, according to Lyria, there very much was. I let her direct me. Those small hands twisted the stems together and handled the petals with such delicate ease I was jealous. For a four year old, she was quite good with her hands, I'd give her that.

I felt a little bad for ruining several of the precious flowers in my misguided attempts to make a crown. But luckily there were more than enough. After a a few false starts and more than a few "no, do it *this* way"s from Lyria, three flower crowns of red and gold sat on the table in front of us.

They weren't perfect, no, but that didn't matter. They were ours.

One for Lyria. One for Nik. One for me.

"We should make one for the baby, too!" Lyria cried suddenly, her eyes wide. "I forgot!"

I chuckled. "The baby isn't even born yet."

"The baby's in Daddy's belly, right? We can just put the crown there!" Before I could say anything else, she grabbed a few more stems and set to work.

Four crowns. Four members of our growing family.

"Papa?" She asked casually as she worked. "How did the baby get in there?"

Good thing I wasn't drinking anything at the moment, cause I nearly choked at those unexpected words. I schooled my features into the best poker face I could. "Magic," I said with a straight face.

"Oh," she said, but gave me that "I don't believe you" face. Thankfully, she didn't press further.

"Ready?" I looked to Lyria, who'd settled her own crown into position. It was a little too big and fell down toward her brows, but even I couldn't deny it looked adorable. The vibrant petals, the delicious scent, and the allegedly magical qualities made it even better.

"You've got to wear yours, too." She handed it to me, her little arms reaching upward but not far enough. I gave a good-natured sigh and ducked my head, and my daughter placed the crown of flowers atop my head.

I was sure I looked ridiculous, but for once I didn't care. I was bonding with my little girl, and we had some flowers to deliver.

———

I ignored the whispers as we made our way across town. We weren't the only ones who'd dressed up. The flower merchant had made his rounds to just about everyone, it seemed, and the air was heavy with floral perfume.

When we approached the healing station the nurse that usually stood watch by the door wasn't there, so we let ourselves in. Nik lay alone on his cot, still drowsing. A blanket covered his midsection, but even so I could see the beginning swell of new life.

We must have looked quite the sight, standing over him with our flower crowns and Lyria carrying two more in her hands. When all was said and done, we were left with one perfect rulo rose. I placed it in a glass by his bedside.

There. A little color.

We spent a few moments in silence, just watching the steady rise and fall of Nik's chest. *Please bring him back to me*, I prayed under my breath, beseeching Glendaria to hear me. *Let us be a family once more.*

I sniffed back a few tears and gestured at Nik's stomach. "You wanna do the honors for the baby crown?"

She placed the tiny red and gold crown on the crest of Nik's stomach. I couldn't help but smile as I thought of what the future would bring. If—no, when—Nik woke up, there would be a new baby on the way. New life, and new beginnings. Not only for this child, but for all of us.

There was still the mystery of the workshop to figure out, sorcerer spies on the loose, and a constant quest to rebuild Darkvale to its former glory, but I remembered one thing Lucien used to say to us all every night we were in exile:

We are Firefangs. And Firefangs mean family.

I had let my mate down once before, but those days were over. I was here now, and I would fight until my dying breath if that's what it took to ensure my family was safe, happy, and loved.

"Last one," Lyria said, her voice wobbly with emotion as she handed me the crown we'd made for Nik. "You do it."

I looked down at the petals in my hand, woven together with the flexible leaves and stems to make a headband of sorts. My mate. My friend. My lover.

He was beautiful now and always. But combining the breathtaking colors of the flower crown as they accentuated the glow of his skin, his hair, his freckles?

It was almost too much to bear.

I leaned forward, holding the crown reverently as if it were a sacred artifact. If this worked, it might as well may be. *Please, Glendaria. Bless us with your holy light.* I mumbled a few more words in the Dragon Tongue of my people before settling the crown to rest over Nik's mussed-up hair.

My dragon roared within me, protective and fierce and very, very alpha. I wanted to wrap my arms and my wings around him and never let go. I wanted to fight off whatever demons he was fighting there inside his mind. I wanted to stand in the way of anything and everything that might hurt him, just because he was mine.

But I couldn't do any of those things. Winds prodded at

my back, desperate for release. My vision flickered and changed back and forth across my dragon sight. Fire built in my chest, smoke filled my nostrils. I needed to shift, needed to protect him, needed to tear limb from limb whatever had hurt him this way.

I felt my daughter at my side, watching with wide, teary eyes. For Lyria, then. And for the babe.

I let out a long, shaky breath. My hands trembled as I gripped the sides of the bed. And then I wept.

"I'm sorry," I whispered as I kissed Nik's forehead.

"I love you," I mumbled as I kissed his nose.

"Now and forever, my mate, my everything." I kissed one cheek, then the other.

"Come back to me," I sobbed, and planted a kiss on those unmoving lips.

When our lips touched, there was more than a spark between us. It was like a bolt of lightning. The tapestry of souls that mates formed together became whole once more. Perhaps Nik had heard us. Perhaps the Goddess had. Who could say?

Nik shuddered, dragging in a hoarse, shaky breath.

Then he sneezed right in my face.

I staggered backward as my heart leapt into my throat. I didn't even have a chance to wipe my face before he sneezed again. And again.

Nik's eyes fluttered open as his body spasmed.

"What's on my head?" He moaned and then sneezed again. "Gnah—I'm allergic—achoo!"

I was still staring at him, mouth hanging open in shock.

And then I laughed. A little chuckle at first, it soon became a roaring, raucous sound. I snatched the crown off his head and tossed it over my shoulder. He was awake, and that was all that mattered.

Lyria leapt on top of him in her joy, wrapping her thin arms around his neck. She'd forgotten to remove her flower crown, though, and Nik started sneezing all over again.

"Seriously," he groaned between sneezes. "Get that stuff away from me!"

I couldn't stop laughing. Tears formed at the corners of my eyes, but they weren't tears of grief this time. Relief, love, amusement, embarrassment, and the irony of the situation flowed through my veins in equal measure. These supposedly magical flowers had woken him up all right—just not in the way we'd expected.

I plucked the crowns off Nik's belly and Lyria's head, discarding them to the side along with the single rose I'd placed on his bedside table. It was just too funny. My chest shook with laughter and joy as I watched Nik try to get his bearings. He was alive. He was awake. And we were all here to greet him.

"Why was there one on my belly?" He mumbled, eyes still squinting against the light. "This was all part of your plot, wasn't it? Wake me with allergies?"

"No," I laughed, brushing a tendril of hair off his forehead. "It was Lyria's idea, actually. She wanted to make you something pretty. And the one on your stomach was for...well, you didn't know? You're pregnant."

Nik's hand shot to his stomach and he felt the small lump there. His face went from confusion to shock to fear to joy in a matter of seconds. "Goddess...the baby...is it all right?"

"I'm sure it is. Your dragon took good care of them, I'm sure."

Nik slumped back into the pillows, closing his eyes again.

"Nurse Meryl! He's awake!"

The omega woman stopped what she was doing and rushed to Nik's bedside, feeling his temple then taking his vitals.

"The baby..." Nik mumbled, still sniffling in the wake of the flowers. "Is the baby okay?"

She ran a hand over his stomach, letting it hover there for a moment. A few seconds later, she smiled. "The baby is healthy."

Nik let out a sigh of relief. "Thank Glendaria."

Thank Glendaria indeed, I repeated in my mind.

"I can't say how, but you've done it." The healer said as she finished her analysis. "He seems to be stable, but we still need to monitor him for a day. I know you're impatient, but he'll be free to go tomorrow."

"I missed you, Daddy," Lyria sniffed, laying her head on Nik's chest. It rose and fell more easily now, and Nik ran a hand through her hair.

"I missed you too, sweetheart." He held her close for several long moments, and Lyria, who'd been so stubbornly strong all this time, finally broke down in gasping sobs.

I leaned over to envelop both of them in my arms. We were one, and nothing would tear us apart again. Not if I had anything to say about it.

As I drew away, not one of us had dry eyes. I sniffed, looking at the ceiling.

Nik turned over on his side with great effort and leveled his gaze at me, suddenly serious. "What happened, Marlowe? I was there with you, and then everything went black, and..."

"You saved my life," I shrugged. "Tork's too. No big deal."

Nik snorted. "Yeah, only you would say saving lives is no big deal." He chewed his lip, considering his next words. "You came back for me."

His eyes were so innocent, shining with that perfect amber glow that melted me from the inside out.

"I will always come back for you, Nik. Now and forever. I know I wronged you in the past. But let's make this a new life, a new day. Just the three—soon, four—of us. Will you give me a chance to be the mate and the father this family needs?" I went to one knee and kissed Nik's hand.

He caught me in those amber eyes again and this time I couldn't look away. Didn't want to. My mate, my omega, the missing piece of my soul. He was alive, and he was mine.

"Yes, Marlowe." Nik said at last. "I will." He stretched his arms toward me. "Now come here!"

Our lips intertwined in one of the most passionate kisses of my life. Into it I poured my grief, my love, my hope. All the pain of the past and the fear of the future melted away. In that moment, we were one.

"Ewww, kissing!" Lyria teased, and I pulled away from my mate, admiring that sleepy expression of joy written all over his face.

We laughed together. Couldn't help it. We were all here. We were family. And we were safe.

21

NIKOLAS

I woke in the middle of the night to the sound of footsteps. I looked around, squinting my eyes against the darkness. The healing ward was eerily silent at night, since most of the daytime healers were gone to be with their families. There were a few on night shift, but much fewer and farther between.

Ever since Nik and Lyria awakened me from that eternal dream world, my strength had returned little by little. I was still weak, sure, but the healers said I was progressing nicely and could go home on the morrow if all things continued well.

So when I heard the sound of sneaky footsteps entering the darkened ward, my ears pricked up.

I tried to sit, but my muscles didn't obey. Not to mention they had me wrapped up in about a million blankets to keep the drafts away. I peeled one to the side, then another.

The hairs on the back of my neck stood up. Someone was behind me. Watching me. I dreaded to turn around and see who it was, until...

It's me, dummy.

I swallowed the lump forming in my throat and whirled around. Marlowe crouched at the edge of my bed, his eyes flitting back and forth as if afraid he'd be spotted.

What are you doing? I hissed at him over our Link.

I had to see you.

I'm fine, I'll be home tomorrow.

Couldn't wait that long. How are you doing? He trailed a hand down my face and I shivered at his touch, my wakening dragon purring with delight. Heat flooded through me where before there was only ice, lighting up the atrophied muscles. Energy and power flooded through our bodies as one and I stared wide-eyed at him, relishing every second.

I need you, Mar... I growled in my mind, pulling him closer. *I thought I was gone, thought you were gone.*

We'll have to be careful, Marlowe raised an eyebrow. *No wrestle fucking, no crying out, and no breaking things this time.*

No promises, I smirked, and pulled him into bed with me. The stiff tiredness fell away in the presence of my mate as his skin, his eyes, his breath lit me up with desire once more. My dragon called out to his, finally together, finally safe. He placed a hand possessively over my stomach, feeling the subtle curve there then dipping lower. I gasped.

No secret babies this time, either, he growled, leaning down to kiss a trail of hot fire down my lips, my neck, my chest, across the swell of my stomach down to my rapidly hardening cock. *This one's all mine.*

I propped myself up to sitting with a few pillows, stuffing the blankets behind me for extra support. Marlowe tilted his head in question as he watched me move, his hands never leaving my flesh. They roamed up and down, wherever they could reach, leaving a shivery electric frisson in their place.

I locked eyes with him. My mate. My alpha. My best friend.

Suck me, I commanded, grabbing a handful of his hair and pulling his face toward me. *Now. Before the healers come back.*

Marlowe's eyes lit up with a possessive fire and he growled just low enough for only the two of us to hear. I fisted my hand in his hair, pulling him onto my cock. His wet, ready lips enveloped my shaft and I threw my head back, sighing breathily.

Uh-uh-uh, Marlowe chastised me in his mind. *Gotta be silent, or no pleasure for you.*

I ground my teeth and curled my toes, taking in a shaky breath through my nose. I could do this.

I call this the thank Goddess you're alive fuck, Marlowe chuckled, and dipped his head lower, suckling the rest of my shaft in one long stroke. His tongue lapped at the underside and head, his cheeks hollow to create a suction as he moved up and down. I guided him with my hand, pulling him closer then pushing him away, using the bed and my hands in his hair for leverage. My hips rocked forward, thrusting into his mouth.

Fuck, I missed this, Marlowe growled.

Missed you more, I shot back.

Challenge accepted, pretty boy. He redoubled his efforts, sucking me off with a passion I'd never seen before. My dragon was burning up, wings tickling at my back and nails lengthening into claws. I bit down on my lip. If I didn't control myself, I'd shift right here.

And that would *definitely* attract attention.

We rocked there together, me fucking his face and Marlowe moving his hands to caress my balls. I felt something tighten within me as I pumped harder, hitting the back of his throat with every thrust.

I was close. Really fucking close.

Don't ever leave me again. I pumped into him mercilessly, Marlowe's gaze never leaving my own. We were locked together in time and space, completely oblivious to anything else but our own pleasures.

Never, he promised, and I couldn't hold it anymore. Everything shattered around me, and I careened over the edge.

I came with a muffled groan that sounded like I was in pain more than pleasure. Breaths came hot and heavy through my nose, my chest heaving as I pumped my load into my mate's mouth, hungry and waiting. And that would have been that, had we not heard the damning sound of a clipboard clattering to the floor.

Marlowe startled at the sound and lost hold of my cock, whirling to see the intruder. I'd already passed the point of no return, though, and cum spurted from my dick in long jets. It splattered into Marlowe's hair, the floor, and the poor nurse's shoes as I watched in horror.

I froze, all the blood rushing straight to my neck and face. Shit. I imagined the harsh sort of reprimand I was in for.

The nurse stood there, fumbling with the buttons on her coat. She stared intently at the ground, unable to meet our gaze. Even in the dim light I could tell she was more than a few shades of red. Absolutely mortified was more like it.

Hell, I was too.

"I was just coming by, to, ahem, check your vitals, Mr. Lastir. But it appears you're doing quite well at the moment." She gave me the most awkward smile I'd ever seen and a nervous, shaky laugh. "Carry on." She winked and turned the corner as fast as possible, leaving us alone again.

As soon as she was out of sight, Marlowe burst into peals of laughter. His chest shook as he lay his head in my lap, wiping a stray tear from his eye.

I reached out a hand to stroke his hair and it came away covered in cum. I grimaced and wiped it on the sheets, which made my mate laugh even harder.

"Come on," he breathed. "That was fucking funny. Did you see that cumshot? That's like world record material, man."

"You're so full of it." I rolled my eyes, but he had a point.

"I think *you're* the one who's full of it." Marlowe waggled his eyebrows. "Or at least...you were."

We held each other and laughed until our sides ached. Whatever. Mates would be mates. It would be a good story, right?

22

NIKOLAS

"You're free to go, Mr. Lastir. May the Goddess be with you." Meryl patted me on the back and gave me a sly wink. Color rushed to my cheeks all over again.

They'd never let me forget that.

I wobbled to my feet and emerged from the healing ward for the first time in what felt like forever. The waning sun cast the world in golden light as I squinted toward the horizon.

Marlowe would have come to meet me but he'd been tied up taking care of Lyria. I couldn't blame him; I was glad he was taking good care of my girl.

But it didn't make it hurt any less.

I gathered my things and set off on foot. Luckily home wasn't far. I reveled in the soft grass and solid ground beneath my feet, drawing in the scent of flowers on the breeze.

What my mate and daughter didn't know was that when I was stuck in that dream-world, when my dragon had pulled away and had taken me along with it, I heard them. I heard every word they said when they thought I was out cold.

Their words and feelings came through like water through a sieve, wrapping around me and arming my soul against the night. I tried to respond, to call out to them, but my voice wouldn't come. I railed against the darkness, shrieking, clawing, sobbing. The pull of the tide was too strong. It pulled me under and locked me away.

Until they put all those blasted flowers in my face, that is.

I heard their words. I felt their love. I experienced their grief.

That's when I knew that what I had with Marlowe was real.

Despite his sometimes cold exterior, Marlowe had a soft gooey center filled with love and longing. I'd always known that, in some way, but there was no better way to tell the character of a man than what he says when he thinks you're not listening.

Not to mention I had teasing ammunition for pretty much forever, now.

I let that thought lift my spirits as I neared the house.

Here's to day one of the rest of your life, I told myself, and opened the door.

————

"Surprise!"

I stopped dead in my tracks. My house was full of my friends and family, leaping up to greet me with smiles on their faces.

I couldn't believe it.

Adrian and Finley were there. Alec, Lucien, Samson, and Corin waved brightly. Thomas and Tork and Myrony and Ansel all made a showing, drinking and laughing and celebrating as they welcomed me home.

I stepped over the threshold and Lyria ran into my arms, throwing herself against me. "Daddy!" She shrieked and wrapped her arms around my neck. I lifted her and hugged her as tight as I could. My little girl was safe.

Marlowe looked on with a grin, arms crossed as he watched each person in the crowd offer their well wishes.

All these people came out here, for me.

I sniffed, my eyes welling with tears as I took in the smiling crowd. After being held hostage for so long...after feeling abandoned, forgotten, unloved...we were all here now. We were all together.

Welcome home, sweetheart, Marlowe spoke in my mind.

Lyria wriggled in my grasp and I let her down as she led me through the throng of people to the kitchen. What I saw there destroyed the last of my resolve to keep from crying.

A tall chocolate cake sat on the table, decorated with intricate icing flowers. Each one was a different color, forming a rainbow around the perimeter. A small paper flag on a toothpick stood in the middle of the cake and below it in curling script was a message:

Welcome home, Nikolas. We love you.

I covered my mouth with my hand and admired the cake closer, sniffing again against the tide of emotion. It was more than delicious-looking, it was a work of art.

Marlowe came to my side, looping an arm around my waist. "What do you think?" He asked.

"Where'd you get so much chocolate?" I said in awe. Chocolate with a prized treat, accessible only in small quantities and at infrequent intervals. And here was a whole cake of it. "It must have cost you a fortune!"

Marlowe's eyes glinted as he pulled me to face him. "I have my ways. And I'll do anything for my mate." He pulled me to him and his lips captured mine, not violent and demanding as they had been the night before, but sensual, passionate, loving. "I love you," Marlowe said against my lips. "Welcome home."

"Glad to be back," I gasped when I found my breath

again. I pulled away to look at the gathering group of people through the doorway. Even more of my old shifter buddies muscled through the door, their eyes lighting up as they saw me for the first time in years.

"To the man that saved my life." Marlowe pushed a drink into my hand. He grabbed something bubbly and raised his glass in my direction. "To my best friend, my omega, my mate."

"Cheers!" The house rumbled with the celebration of human and shifter alike.

I took a long sip with the rest of my friends and family, smiling at the delightfully fizzy nectar.

"Speech!" Tork clapped, jostling his mug in the process. "Speech!"

I scoffed, my face growing red again as everyone's eyes watched me. Gosh, I didn't know I was gonna have to make a speech! I took a deep breath and addressed the crowd.

"My friends, my family. My clan. Thank you all for being here. It warms my heart more than I can say that you've chosen to celebrate here with me today. When my dragon retracted, I saw what some might call The Great Beyond. I could reach out and touch it. I thought I was dead. But the Goddess decided my time on this world is not done just yet. When I was there I heard voices cutting through the darkness. I heard my daughter. I heard my mate. The last few years have been difficult. Many things have changed. When Darkvale fell I lost everything. I didn't believe in second chances. But I've never been so proud to be wrong in all my days, and I'm truly blessed to have this man as my mate. To Marlowe, everyone!"

"To Marlowe!" The clan roared in agreement. I had my mate and my girl by my side, my friends all around me, and a little one on the way.

It was the best day of my life.

23

MARLOWE

Two weeks later

"You may enter," I said without looking up. Weeks after Nik had returned from the healing ward, I was still buried in diplomatic bullshit.

The door opened and Elias stepped through, joined by one of my guards. I looked up when I saw the flow of his robes across the floor.

I didn't want to admit it, but Elias had become quite the asset. Despite his cantankerous personality he was smart as hell, and knew how to get information we couldn't by ourselves. I'd tasked him with analyzing the findings from the underground workshop we'd discovered, and I could only assume he was here now to share his results.

"Elias," I said, bowing my head slightly. "Sit down."

The Sorcerer swept his robes behind him and sat, the guard still standing vigil by his side.

"You may leave us, Kaine. I wish to speak to Elias alone."

Kaine hesitated. "Yes, Commander," He said at last, leaving with a short bow.

"Now," I leaned forward at my desk, considering him over my steepled fingers. "What news have you brought me?"

Elias fished a scroll out of one of the voluminous pockets of his robes. I gestured for him to bring it forward.

He removed the metal ring holding it in place and spread out the crumpled paper on the table. Scratches of ink and calculations littered the page, along with some foreign language I'd never seen before. What I did recognize, however, was the eerie replication of the discarded metal limbs I'd seen in the workshop. Only, they weren't disembodied anymore. Elias had added on a torso, arms, and even a head. What I saw could only be described as a "metal man."

"What is this about?" I said softly, my breath catching in my throat. The thought of that metal coming to life...I shivered. I may be a dragon, but to animate lifeless metal? I couldn't imagine the amount of power that would take.

"I've inspected each of the artifacts recovered from this workshop of yours. It's quite incredible, I've never seen readings like these before."

"But what does it mean?" I pressed him. "We need to know what we're up against. We need to keep Darkvale safe."

Elias pursed his lips. "I don't know." His shoulders slumped over the parchment. "I've been trying to figure out how it's even possible, but…"

"Try harder." I commanded, leaning back in my chair. "The fate of our people is at stake."

"Yes, Commander," he bowed his head. "I will do my best, but I need more resources."

I gazed at him. Of course he did.

"I'll contact the magitech engineers and send one along with you. Will that be enough?"

"It's a start, but this is complicated stuff." Elias wrung his hands. "I think I'm on to something big, but I need more time."

I drew in a deep breath.

"Time you will have, Sorcerer, but if I get even the faintest hint of foul play…"

"You have my word. That still stands from before."

I considered his proposition. True, he hadn't led us astray yet. In fact, quite the opposite. Maybe all Sorcerers weren't so bad, after all.

"Am I free to go?" He asked at length. "I need to get back

to my studies."

"Leave." I waved him away.

Without a word he gathered up his papers, refastening them carefully, then exited through the double doors.

I let out a breath and ran a hand through my hair when he was gone.

What in Glendaria's name were they working on? And *who* was 'they', for that matter? The Paradox? The humans? Or someone else entirely?

If they were even close to building a mechanized warrior like in Elias's drawings, we were in a lot more danger than I thought.

Especially if that kind of technology fell into the wrong hands.

I was making a note to report this news to Lucien when I heard Nik's voice in my mind.

Dinner's almost ready. You about done over there?

Yeah, I mindspoke back to him. *I'll be right there.*

My stomach growled as I stood up from my desk. I'd been so caught up with meetings and paperwork all day I had barely eaten anything. Even from here I could smell the delicious scent of the night's clan dinner.

After a full belly of food and the company of my mate and daughter, things would look brighter. They had to.

24

MARLOWE

Two months later

"Ugh, I feel like a balloon." Nik fell backwards into the bed with a thump. He was quite pregnant now, the swell of his stomach forming a graceful arch from his torso down to his legs. It didn't look easy to carry that much extra weight around. I couldn't have done it, that was for sure.

"Why don't you rest?" I suggested and kissed his forehead. "I've already told the Council I'm not coming in until after the baby's born. Should be any day now." I grinned and caressed Nik's stomach, still marveling at the smooth, round shape and how well it fit in my hands. I leaned down to kiss him there and I got a kick to the face from the little one. It wasn't very hard, but I could definitely feel it.

"Ouch," I joked, rubbing my cheek. "Your baby is feisty."

"You have no idea," Nik rolled his eyes. "Keeping me up at all hours of the night, running to the bathroom every hour on the hour...and don't even get me started on the swollen ankles."

I rubbed his back in small circles, focusing on the tense muscles there. "It will all be over soon."

"Yeah, and then the hard part begins—actually being parents."

"It's difficult, sure," I admitted. "But we're in this together. And I'm sure the baby will be just as strong and beautiful as you are." I kissed his shoulder and held him close to me.

Nikolas let out a sigh and turned away. I thought I could detect the hint of a blush there.

"What?" I asked softly.

Nik mumbled something too low for me to hear. He was a bright beet red now, which made me even more curious.

"What's the matter?" I asked again.

"I miss feeling you inside me," he mumbled and hid his face in the pillows.

I stared at him, mouth open. Between work and time with Lyria, neither of us had had much time or energy to be intimate. And with the fatigue and swelling from Nik's pregnancy, I falsely assumed he wouldn't want to.

How wrong I was.

"You'd want me to...like this?" I caressed his stomach and kissed my way down his back, leaving gooseflesh there.

Nik rolled over and caught my gaze. "Why not?" His eyes glittered with need, and my dragon couldn't resist.

Still, I tried to keep a handle on my feelings. Protecting my mate and my baby was most important, even if I did want to pound him into the mattress.

"I'm not gonna...I dunno, hurt the baby?" My heart had already started going double-time, and blood rushed to my cock as I thought of fucking my pregnant mate.

"We'll just have to be gentle. Here, lay behind me. We can spoon."

"What about Lyria?" I cocked my head toward the hallway. She was sound asleep in the next room, and if she was going to stay that way, we'd need to be quiet.

"She sleeps like a rock. You've seen her. Come on." Nik stroked my neck and I closed my eyes, tilting my head back.

"Okay," I said shakily, but my dragon was already raring to go.

Nik didn't know what he was talking about when he said he felt gross and ugly. Nothing could be further from the truth. He positively glowed with pregnancy, and he was carrying my child. Nothing could be hotter than that.

I positioned myself behind him, one arm behind my head while the other wrapped around his torso. I put a hand protectively on his belly and kissed his shoulder again. "This okay?"

"Yeah."

I rubbed my rapidly hardening cock against his back and Nik responded in kind, moving back and forth with me in a steady, slow motion.

"That feels good," Nik sighed. "Want more."

I used my free hand to snake down to the curve of his ass. Goddess, he was so wet already. My fingers came away coated in his slick juices and I brought them to my nose.

The scent of him drove my dragon wild. I nearly vibrated with need but held myself back. "Tell me if I'm being too rough."

"I will. I'm not made of glass, you know."

Wasn't that the truth. "Far from it," I agreed as I aligned my cock with his opening. "You are the strongest, kindest, bravest omega I've ever met. And I'm honored to have you as my mate." I pressed into him gently as I said each word, inch by delicious inch until I was buried to the hilt.

Nik made a soft choking moan, rocking against me. A sigh of pleasure, of relief, almost.

His warm, tight walls gripped my cock and shot sparks of

pleasure up and down my spine. I wrapped my arm around him again and pulled him even closer, desperate for connection.

With a slow, tortured rocking of my hips, I drew out of him, listening to Nik's shuddered gasps. His body twitched with each passionate thrust, shivering and shaking in my arms.

"Goddess, you're so fucking hot." I growled next to his ear. "You're gonna make me come just from the sounds you make."

Nik blushed again and gave me an embarrassed grin. "I can't help it," he mumbled with hooded eyes. "You feel so good."

"So do you," I replied, capturing his lips in a kiss as I drove into him again.

This time as we joined together, it was more than a feral clash of bodies. It was more than a reckless pursuit of pleasure. We gave and took, rocking into one another with a slow, passionate rhythm that drove each breath, each sigh, each beat of our hearts. It was a glowing ember of sensuality instead of a fiery explosion.

And everyone knows that embers burn hottest.

It was a slow ascent that took over each of our bodies and souls, keeping us locked in the moment and completely at one with one another. It consumed me from head to toe as I pressed into him again and again, picking up the pace and possessively stroking Nik's pregnant belly.

My mate. My lover. My baby.

My breathing became labored and my thrusts quickened as I clung to Nik for dear life. My balls tightened, edged to the point of insanity. And then I broke down, shuddering and coming deep inside his channel as we shook and spasmed in each other's arms. My knot swelled within him and held us there, locked together in our passion, as Nik turned his head and eyed me with a sleepy, sated gaze.

"I love you, Marlowe."

"I love you too, Nik."

We lay there, joined as alpha and omega, until our breathing slowed and sleep came for us both.

———

I woke the next morning to a panicked yelp coming from the bathroom.

All vestiges of sleep left me in an instant. My eyes shot open, my dragon ready to pounce.

"What's wrong?" I called, my voice still hoarse from sleep.

Nik's muffled voice came from the other side of the door. "My water broke! And I'm cramping like crazy!"

Oh, Goddess. I sat bolt upright in bed, my head spinning. The baby was coming. The baby was finally coming!

"Stay calm!" I called through the door, as much to myself as to him. "Can you come out here?"

"I think so," he groaned and the door opened. Nik emerged in a robe. His face was a pale white and he clamped a hand over his stomach, wincing.

I felt fear greater than any battle. My mate was hurting, and I had to do something!

I spread a blanket out over the bed and eased him down onto it. "Stay right here, I'll get the doctor."

"As if I could get very far," Nik grimaced. "I blame you for this! You're the one that had to go and shake things up in there last night." His eyes were alight with mischief and it took me a few seconds to figure out what he was talking about.

"Ohhh..." I groaned. Excitement and fear washed through me in equal measure.

This was it.

I was thrilled to be there for my mate and see the new addition to our family, but what if I messed it up? What if I wasn't a good father after all? I'd had some practice with Lyria, but this was a *baby*.

My protective instincts won over and spurred me into

action. I nearly tripped over the bundle of clothes on the floor when I heard Lyria from the other room.

"What's going on?" She emerged from her room in a nightgown, still rubbing the sleep from her eyes.

I knelt down to her at eye level. "You're gonna be a big sister, soon. The baby is coming, and Daddy needs you to watch over him while I go get the doctor. Can you do that for Papa?"

"Is he gonna be okay?" She warbled, those innocent eyes worried.

"He will be okay. I promise." I drew her into a hug. "I'll be right back. Don't go anywhere until I return."

I heard Lyria rush into Nik's room, shouting at top of her lungs. "BABY! ARE YOU IN THERE?"

I choked out a laugh, then got to my feet and ran.

———

Not ten minutes later I returned with Doctor Parley and his assistant Anna in tow. One look at Nik's pained face and he turned to me.

"Usually we do deliveries in the medical ward, but the baby's coming now. Little bugger is persistent. There's no time."

"What does that mean?" I croaked, my heart hammering against my chest.

"We'll have to make do," he said, and snapped on a pair of gloves.

I hovered around the room, watching with wide eyes as Dr. Parley and Anna rushed about, propping Nik up on a pile of pillows and pulling a blanket over his lower half. I held Lyria as she buried her face in my shirt.

Nik yelped again and clenched at his stomach. It took all my willpower not to run to him and grab his hand.

The doctor twisted his lips and gave a weary shake of his head. "We're gonna need to do a C-section."

"What?" I screamed, and this time I actually did lunge forward. "You can't!"

"Mr. Marlowe," the doctor scolded, pushing me away. "If you can't keep your wits about you, you'll have to leave. Your mate is in good hands but only if you leave me and my assistant to do our work. What will it be?"

My dragon heated up, ready to let him taste my fire, then Nik reached out and grabbed my hand. He gave me a tired smile. "Hey. Don't worry about me."

"I always worry about you," I admitted.

"Take Lyria and wait outside. I'll be okay. I promise."

I took a long last look into his eyes and squeezed his hand. "You better be."

Lyria looked at me and then at Nik with wide, worried

eyes. "I'll be all right, sweetheart." Nik soothed her. "Go with Papa. Your baby brother is coming."

"Brother?" I raised an eyebrow. "How do you know?"

"I don't," Nik shrugged, then groaned again as another contraction hit him. "Just a hunch. The way this one's been kicking? Definitely an alpha, and probably a boy too."

"Clear the room," the doctor commanded. "We need to get started."

I love you, I sent to Nikolas over our Link.

I love you too.

I took Lyria's hand and left the room, but it felt like I left a piece of my soul behind.

————

I paced back and forth, back and forth. Lyria sat in a chair and watched as I chewed my lip, fidgeted, clenched and unclenched my fists. Sweat beaded up on my forehead and I could barely think straight. Every fiber in my being screamed at me to barge back in there and protect my mate, but I could not. The doctors knew what they were doing, and Dr. Parley was right. I'd only get in the way.

Lyria dangled her legs off the chair and sat silently, but I could hear all her worries in my mind. Trying to soothe myself and her at the same time was a hell of a job.

She started talking, perhaps to distract herself from her fear, but it helped me calm down as well.

"I didn't like you at first," She admitted. "But you take good care of Daddy."

I scoffed at her candor. At least she'd come around. "I do my best."

"Are you gonna stay with us, Papa?" She clung to my sleeve. The idea that she'd even had to worry about that broke my heart, so I wrapped my arms around her and pulled her into a hug.

"I'm not going anywhere. Papa is here to stay. I'm sorry I was gone before, but I'm gonna be the best Papa ever from now on. Give me a chance?"

Lyria nodded and buried her head in my chest again. *I love you, iskra. I'll never leave you again.*

A cry came from the next room and startled us both. I leapt up, ready to attack. But that cry wasn't a cry of pain. No.

It was a high-pitched, gasping cry of new life.

My heart nearly stopped right then and there.

A spark of life jolted through our Link, branching off from my mate's connection into a new one all its own. Another branch in our growing family tree.

A moment later Anna returned, wiping her hands on a

towel. "You can come in now," she beamed at Lyria. "Come see your new baby sister."

"Sister?" Lyria cried, and ran into the room.

I followed her and the sight took my breath away.

Nik lay in bed, flushed and exhausted, but happier than I'd ever seen him. He held a screeching baby in his arms and a smile on his face. I stood in awe of how small she was.

Lyria covered her ears. "How is something that small so loud!?"

Boy, was she in for a surprise.

I chuckled and led her to the bed where the baby quieted for a blessed second. It was almost as if she felt our presence. Her wide amber eyes latched onto mine and I felt the reverberation of our dragon souls mingling.

"Hey there," I cooed. "I'm your Papa, and this is your big sister."

"Hey, baby." Lyria still stood back a bit, ready to cover her ears again at the next screech.

How are you doing? I asked Nik in mindspeak.

Tired, he responded. *But look at her*.

I couldn't take my eyes away from our new child. She was the most beautiful thing I'd ever seen.

A storm still gathered over Darkvale, but that didn't matter at the moment. As long as we had each other, we could weather any obstacle. We had friends, family, and allies on our side.

"She's everything I could ever wish for, and more." Nik mused without taking his eyes off our girl. "I've got my mate, two beautiful girls, and an entire clan at our backs."

"What should we call her?" I asked Nik, gently brushing back the tiny tuft of hair on the baby's head. She whimpered again and wobbled her arms and legs, clinging close to her Daddy's warmth.

"I have an idea," Lyria piped up, and we both looked at her.

"What's that?" I figured she would come up with some silly, out of place answer, and I was already concocting a careful reply when she spoke.

"How about Hope?"

Hope. I repeated the word and looked at Nik. His eyes shone with what could have been tears.

Hope was what got me from the trenches of warfare back into my mate's arms. Hope was what won back our homeland from the intruders. And hope was what would carry us into the future, come what may.

"It's perfect." I said, and Nik agreed.

"Hope it is," Nik said, snuggling her close to him. He kissed our daughter's forehead, and closed his eyes to rest.

We were together.

We were family.

We were Firefangs.

And nothing would stand in our way.

AUTHOR'S NOTE

Thank you so much for picking up this book! I hope you've come to enjoy the world and the characters of Darkvale just as much as I have.

If you have a moment, consider leaving a review on Amazon. It helps more people find books they love.

Book 3 will be called The Dragon's Forbidden Omega. Keep an eye out for it soon!

May all your fires burn bright,

— Connor Crowe

When the kids are away, the mates will play...
Sign up here for your FREE copy of ONE KNOTTY
NIGHT, a special story that's too hot for Amazon!
https://dl.bookfunnel.com/c1d8qcu6h8

Facebook:
fb.me/connorcrowempreg

62065632R00145

Made in the USA
Columbia, SC
28 June 2019